TREMBLE + ENNUI

a novel by Edgar Nicaud

D1240210

COATPOCKET
PRESS

Library of Congress Control Number: 2005907505

ISBN: 097685740-5

Cover photograph of New Orleans
rooftops in 2005 by Cissy Rowley.

Special thanks to
Julie Mazur, Diana Grumbles,
and the Gossards.

Printed in the U.S.A.

CoatPocket Press
New Orleans, Louisiana

www.coatpocket.com

Author's Note

I am from New Orleans, where my family has been for six generations. At one time I was a banker here, but I got tired of being a banker, so I quit and wrote this book. Then I went on to do other things.

Seven years later, and a few days ago, Tremble + Ennui was about to be sent to the printer when the hurricane put the city and my house under water. The New Orleans I know is gone, for better and for worse.

I thought about whether I should change this book. But how? Perhaps it is best to leave something that is a reflection of what New Orleans once was.

So I didn't change a word, and instead am writing this note. I hope you understand.

Edgar Nicaud
September 2005

TREMBLE + ENNUI

THE HIGH LIFE

Tremble and Ennui
deal with
reduced circumstances

They were a nice enough young couple. Her name was Tremble and his was Ennui. They lived on Soraparu Street, in the city of New Orleans.

Soraparu was a street like so many in that wasted town. It was a dirt road crowded with shotgun houses, existing behind the avenues of rotting mansions. Each little house had a screen door and a porch. On each porch was a beer-drinking old man in a rusted chair, or a mother surrounded by a mob of children. Some of the houses were still decorated with victorian gingerbread, but most had been stripped bare by various neighborhood entrepreneurs.

Although the street was not among the more desirable in the city, it had its benefits. Much to Tremble's delight, each month she found a welfare check in the mail, addressed to a previous tenant with seven children. Tremble was able to cash the check at a steep discount through one of several young men who were always standing around.

As for Ennui, he learned from his neighbors how to obtain a steady supply of food stamps, which he used to purchase morbidly large inventories of top-shelf gin and vermouth at the corner store.

There were other advantages to living where they did. Tremble and Ennui's numerous creditors didn't dare come near for fear of being shot, stabbed, beaten or robbed. Nosy friends from the past with disapproving looks wouldn't dream of dropping by. And in addition to the rent being scandalously cheap, the landlord seemed shocked, or even offended if it was paid on time.

They wake
and
have breakfast

One afternoon Tremble woke up and tried to dress, only to find that everything made her breasts look small. She stood in front of the mirror and stared at them, and they stared back.

"Are my breasts large?" she asked Ennui, who was still in bed. He was covered by several outfits Tremble had discarded.

"Of course," said Ennui.

Tremble reflected that Ennui was like a fossil under layers of rock. Surely there was some meaning to this, but she was too hung over to grasp it. So her thoughts turned back to her breasts.

"They don't look big," Tremble said crossly. "The only thing big is my ass. I knew I shouldn't have eaten yesterday."

She disappeared into the bathroom for a few minutes and there was only the sound of running water. When she came out she looked in the mirror. "Much better."

Tremble walked her girlish figure around the high-ceilinged house, trying on one thing and then another. Finally, she put on her black Chanel suit.

Ennui slid out from under the clothes and looked himself over. He was still wearing his dead grandfather's smoking jacket and cuff links, a satisfactory outfit. He crawled to the kitchen and shook a few things and made himself a martini. Sitting on the floor, he held the drink just so between his thumb and finger and smacked his lips contentedly and said "ah" after each sip.

"Aren't you going to make me breakfast?" Tremble demanded. She was standing over him and tapping her shoe.

"I'm sorry, have mine," said Ennui.

Tremble took the drink. "If you're going to lounge around until I meet a wealthy husband, at least you can serve me in the best way you can. I would throw you out, except you make excellent martinis."

Marriage benefits
are discussed

After Ennui finished a few drinks, he began thinking clearly. "Ah, your funeral outfit again," he said.

"What do you mean, again?" said Tremble.

"You wore it last week."

Tremble stomped over to the sofa and flung herself on it with a dramatic sigh. "I know, I know, everything is just so boring these days. It's the same thing over and over."

"Perhaps we should try something different."

"Don't try to talk me into getting married again, Ennui," Tremble moaned. "We're just not meant to be married."

"Because I'm dry on funds?"

"No, people don't marry for money."

"Sex?"

"Don't be ridiculous. Married couples rarely have sex. And they never have it with each other."

"Beauty, then."

"Don't be shallow."

"What's wrong with being shallow? A martini is a shallow drink, much to its advantage."

"Don't change the subject."

"What was the subject?"

"Marriage, stupid." Tremble shuddered and made a rude face. "Everybody knows that people only marry so they can have an excuse to get drunk. How else could one face the horrors of marriage? We're already drunk every day, so I can't see the point."

"I see," said Ennui. "No, actually I don't. Perhaps a drink would help. Would you like another?"

"Yes, but a little dryer this time my dear. Wet martinis are for old people."

Tremble calls
her friend Bertel

After Tremble and Ennui had finished a few martinis they talked about what to do for the day.

"How about a nice walk around the park," said Ennui.

"Only sober or overweight people walk around the park," said Tremble. "We are neither."

"A shopping spree?"

"Our credit cards have all been confiscated and sliced in two."

"Perhaps we should look for jobs then."

"And work!"

"What was I thinking?"

"I fear dementia is setting in with you," said Tremble.

She pulled herself up and paced around the tiny house. "I know," she finally said. "We'll go drinking."

"Excellent idea," said Ennui. He downed his martini and smiled broadly. "I don't know why I didn't think of it myself. It has proven to be the best thing to do every day for as long as I can remember."

"As my daddy always said, you must build success upon success," Tremble declared.

"Sound advice."

"And we must go to Intesti's. We'll need to arrive in a nice car, or they'll never run us a tab. I'll call Bertel."

"Bertel Milksop?" Ennui spat out. "I can't be seen in the company of a hairy animal like that."

"Don't get pouty this early in the afternoon," said Tremble. She patted Ennui's head. "Bertel has been so annoying lately, trying to make me ride in his new Cadillac."

Tremble called Bertel and talked to him as though he was the best person in the world. Moments later, Bertel was out front honking frantically.

"I can't wait," cried Tremble. "Intesti's makes the best martinis."

Ennui frowned and looked sad.

"Except for yours of course," Tremble added.

Ennui smiled and brightened. "Yes, of course."

Bertel meets
the neighbors

Bertel was standing proudly in front of his car. Unlike him, it was a beautiful thing.

Some years back, Bertel had gotten in with the wrong set of clothes. He wore khaki trousers, a faded madras shirt, and ruined penny loafers. Oddly, there was a small portrait of a duck's head sewn just above his ass. His belly—a legacy from drinking light beer every night during his fraternity days—looked out over his leather-weave belt.

"Are we safe in this neighborhood?" Bertel asked, as some neighbors began to gravitate toward the shiny car, like ants to food. He looked around as though someone was holding a rotten banana under his nose.

"Oh, Bertel, you are so sweet to be concerned about my safety," said Tremble. "And look, the children of the neighborhood are coming to greet you. How darling."

An ambitious young man approached and asked Bertel a question. "He just asked me if I was hiring," Bertel snorted.

Ennui climbed into the back seat. It was spacious and comfortable, and made him feel like a captain of industry.

As he was settling in, a commotion began outside. A white Lincoln with gold trim and curb feelers had pulled up to Bertel's car.

"Who the hell is that?" Bertel said.

"Don't be so dramatic," said Tremble. "One of the neighbors thinks you're trying to acquire his turf." She climbed into the passenger seat and closed the door.

A muscular man who had not yet grown into his pants exited the Lincoln and said, "You trying to eat up my block?"

"This discussion may become animated," said Ennui. "I'd hate to spill my drink. This *is* a Sedan de Ville, you know. Perhaps I should lock the doors."

"Whatever you think." Tremble yawned and checked her hair in the mirror.

There was a loud banging on the window. It was Bertel. He was trying to get in but his turf rival kept grabbing his head and pounding it against the hood.

"Can't your friend quiet down," said Ennui. "I was drifting into a most pleasant stupor, reflecting on a movement in Handel's *Messiah*, and now this."

"I suppose we should let him in," said Tremble. "He's damaging the hood."

Tremble leaned over and unlocked the door. With a shriek, Bertel scrambled inside the car and they sped away. Gunfire sounded behind them.

Bertel was hyperventilating and his clothes were torn badly, but otherwise he seemed to have escaped unscathed.

"Bertel," sighed Tremble, "you should spend less time discussing luxury cars with other enthusiasts and pay more attention to me. Ennui, see if you can find a bag for Bertel to breathe into."

"And let the sunlight strike my bottle of gin?" Ennui replied. "I think not."

Society's problems
are touched upon

Once Bertel stopped hyperventilating, he began to complain about crime in the city.

"You may have a point," said Ennui. "There are quite a number of prostitutes around."

"And plenty of drunks as well," said Tremble.

Bertel said it was the fault of welfare. "Welfare moms breed criminals who harass people like me."

"I can't blame welfare mothers," said Tremble. "I mean, goodness, who would want to work."

"I don't care where they work," cried Bertel, "but they've got to. They can wash dishes for all I care."

Tremble laughed. "Dishwashing, Bertel? How animalistic. Really, there's no need to be primitive."

Bertel was grabbing at his rump, and his hand came up empty. "He ripped off my duck!" he bawled, as the car bounded over potholes and entered downtown.

The restaurant takes care of Bertel

"Oh, good," said Tremble. "Here we are. We'll be valet parking, of course."

They pulled up to Intesti's. Valets leapt forward and opened the doors for Ennui and Tremble. Ennui emerged with much dignity and magnificence. He was wearing his smoking jacket, fine slacks, antique cuff links, and tasseled loafers. He stepped out of the car holding his martini perfectly upright, like a scepter.

"My driver is so out of sorts today," Tremble whispered into the valet's ear. "He arrived this afternoon reeking of beer, and dressed like a bum. Terrible, isn't it—the help you get these days. He's so drunk he may try to come in—please don't let him in under any circumstances. And by all means don't take the car."

The valet eyed Bertel's horrible clothing and nodded, understanding.

"I'm afraid they are all out of valet parking," said Tremble to Bertel. "Please be a sweetie and park the car, will you? We'll be inside and will get you a drink. There's bound to be parking just around the corner."

Bertel began to complain but Tremble gave him a look and he obeyed. The Cadillac crept away.

"Thank gawd," groaned Ennui. "Tell me he is gone for good."

"We *are* downtown," said Tremble. "It will take him at least an hour to find parking. I don't know why he was such a stickler about not letting the valet park his car. He is so strange."

"And that outfit of his, completely vomitous. Especially with the tears in the shirt. Isn't that out of style?"

"I don't know, my darling Ennui. And vomitous? Where do you get your vocabulary?"

Ennui and Tremble walked arm in arm into Intesti's. The door was opened before them and they smelled the delicious foods and beheld the waiters scurrying to and fro. They both sighed.

"Ah, Intesti's," said Ennui.

"Intesti's, wrap yourself around me," said Tremble.

Tremble suddenly realized she was hungry. She had not planned on eating today, but she never actually planned on eating. She only had moments of weakness.

"Let's have some food," she declared.

"But how will we pay for it?" said Ennui. Intesti's just happened to be the city's most expensive restaurant.

"Oh Ennui." Tremble patted his arm. "We never pay for anything. We don't have any money, remember? Therefore how could we pay?"

"Yes, right. Forgive me. These martinis tend to impair my memory."

Ennui
orders wine

Walking in as they did—drunk, obnoxious and oddly dressed—the hostess assumed that Tremble and Ennui had to be either wealthy or famous. Her suspicion was confirmed when she asked the couple if they had reservations, to which Ennui sniffed in disgust, "Of course not, silly girl, do we look like the sort of people who would make reservations here?"

As a result, they were immediately seated at the restaurant's best table.

The waiter approached and after some initial pleasantries began to explain a special. "Spray-painted in a lemon-butter sauce with—"

Ennui waved his hand dismissively. "Please, please," he said. "If it is not written down it doesn't concern me."

"Don't be rude," said Tremble.

"I'm not being rude," said Ennui. "I'm merely trying to educate the servants. Please observe."

Ennui turned to the waiter. "Right now I should be tasting my appetizer and enjoying a glass of your finest wine, not trying to decipher your idiotic banter that only impresses idiots. I don't want to know how the food is cooked. I just want it cooked well. I am not a cook nor by god do I want to learn how to cook. It would be the equivalent of wanting to know how my mechanic tuned up my Cadillac. Now scurry along and bring us a list of your fine wines."

The waiter reddened noticeably and ran off.

Tremble looked on in admiration. "Ennui, you are so eloquent today."

"I thought you said I was rude," he said.

"Well I changed my mind. You are eloquently rude."

"I'd much rather be rudely eloquent."

"I'd much rather be rudely drunk."

"Cheers to that," said Ennui. He finished his martini and looked around for another.

A different waiter appeared with the wine list. Ennui flipped through it with contempt and threw it on the floor.

"I asked for a list of your fine wines, not a survey of rot-gut available in the discount bin of a supermarket. Now scamper back and bring me the list."

"I'm sorry, sir, this is our wine list. If it is not acceptable—"

"Enough of this nonsense. Surely a place with a reputation such as this would be embarrassed to offer people such as us these vomitous wines!"

"Vomitous, sir?"

"Exactly," said Tremble. "Now listen to Ennui and run along. He's in fine form today."

The waiter hurried away.

"I fear I am getting drunk and opinionated," said Ennui.

Tremble grabbed his hand. "My dear Ennui," she said. "You always know how to handle these situations."

A few moments later the sommelier himself arrived, ruddy and irritated. "Now what would you suggest, sir," he asked.

"Perhaps a bottle of Saint d'Infection Enflammée, 1968," said Ennui.

"We judged it too tannic for our tastes," sniffed the sommelier.

"Then Château Idiot Ravi, vintages 1974, 1977, or 1981,"

"All the pre-1978 vintages became vinegary, and 1981 is still too young."

"Saint Dément Moroneric."

"Impossible! Overrated!"

"Then what is your most expensive wine?"

The man consulted the book. "Château Facilment Impressioné. $325 per bottle!"

"I suppose we can suffer though it," said Ennui. "Bring it and continue to bring a bottle every time ours is half empty."

"Yes *sir*," said the sommelier. He turned on his heel and marched away.

"I didn't know you knew anything about wines," said Tremble.

"I don't," said Ennui.

Chef Intesti appears
to his patrons

Tremble and Ennui were given menus. They proceeded to order the most expensive items because they didn't trust the less expensive ones, believing them to be inferior. Consequently, all sorts of rare animal parts began to arrive at their table, some flamed, some sautéed, some oven-exploded according to the creative orgy for which Chef Intesti was known worldwide. A murmur arose throughout the restaurant, as lesser patrons observed what was obviously a rare display of the ability to eat.

Tremble was happy and she kept squeezing Ennui's knee. Ennui squeezed Tremble's knee as well but his hand kept climbing only to be slapped by Tremble and noted by a giggle.

"Are you sure you don't have any money?" said Tremble.

"Positively," said Ennui. "I am extremely talented at spending money. Much more so than people who actually have it. But I have no interest in obtaining money—other than the only civilized way, which is to inherit it, of course."

"Such a shame. Otherwise we should marry immediately."

Tremble gazed fondly at Ennui and Ennui gazed fondly at Tremble. He lifted a fork of Arizona range-fed lobster scorched over a redwood tree-flamed grill and fed this into Tremble's young lips.

"Oh, Ennui," she said. "Chef Intesti is truly a master."

She lifted a chunk of trash-can fire roasted bald eagle marinated in a sauce of whale oil and fed this into Ennui's eager mouth.

"The best chef in the world," he said.

They toasted and gulped down the last of their fourth bottle of wine.

Just then Chef Intesti appeared, in all his majesty, to behold this young couple, these ardent disciples of his cooking, who should be an example to all. This was a great chef—he had his own television show, a line of cookbooks, branches of his restaurants in popular tourist destinations, and his company listed on the New York

Stock Exchange. In addition, he smelled vaguely like cut cheese.

In his presence, Tremble sat wide-eyed and open-mouthed, a posture which ignited the flames of the Chef's desire.

"How's that food hittin your insides," Chef Intesti grunted. He looked shorter and greasier than he did on his television show.

"Wonderfully," exhaled Tremble. Her chest heaved in young, potent admiration.

"Not quite up to what we're used to at the house, of course," said Ennui, "but passable for restaurant food."

Tremble kicked Ennui under the table. He stuck out his tongue at her.

"You are truly a master of your tools," Tremble murmured to the Chef.

Chef Intesti reddened a touch. Who was this saucy wench, looking to be put on a spit and roasted?

"Well, hope you enjoys eatin it," he said. He handed her a card. "Here yous go. It good for a tour of my kitchen." Then he departed.

Tremble looked bleary-eyed at the card.

"I suppose he'll want to show you his tool," said Ennui.

"Oh shut up Ennui," said Tremble. "You're being quite the tool. Chef Intesti has a culinary empire. What do you have? An excellent martini recipe and that's about it."

"I also have good cuff links."

"Okay, you have good cuff links as well. But that isn't enough to marry on."

"So you are going to marry that grubby, squatty Chef Intesti? He's more of an animal than Bertel."

"You really grate on me," Tremble cried. "And what is that racket?"

Bertel joins
the party
and pays

That racket was Bertel, who was unable to gain admittance to Intesti's. He had been banging at the window for some time before Tremble and Ennui noticed. His eyes were large and bloodshot. His face was red and swollen like a fat beet and his hair looked like it had exploded.

"I believe I have seen that person before," said Ennui. "But where?"

"He drove us here you drunkard," cried Tremble. "Just shut up and tell the hostess to let him in."

"Yes, of course. But meanwhile you might want to think about the bill."

Ennui went off sheepishly and came back a few minutes later. Bertel was livid. "The valets wouldn't let me in," he gasped. "I've been out there fighting with them for over an hour."

"Well it's a good thing you weren't arrested for vagrancy," said Ennui.

"I had to park a mile away, all the way out on Tchoupitoulas," Bertel cried. "I have never been treated like this—like an animal."

"Now now, Bertel," said Tremble. She pulled her chair close to his and stroked his hair tenderly. "You're hungry and cranky, just like a little baby. Have some wine and we'll get you some food."

"We are already deep into our fourteenth course," snapped Ennui. "The whole delicate rhythm of the meal has been thrown off."

"Would you please shut up!" cried Tremble. "Just go find Bertel's car. It should take you at least a half-hour, which I desperately need after suffering through your company. I would like more than anything in the world to spend some time alone with my good friend Bertel."

"I don't think he's okay to drive," Bertel ventured.

"Of course he is," said Tremble. "You should see him sober. He shakes like a leaf."

Tremble slid her hand into Bertel's pocket and took the keys, which she handed to Ennui. "Now scat!"

After Ennui left, Tremble proceeded to drink several glasses of wine with Bertel and to stroke all three of his legs under the table. Bertel got some food and began to feel better. Tremble gazed so lovingly in his eyes and she looked so innocent that all was soon forgotten. Before long he was laughing and smiling and telling incredibly dull stories about work.

Ennui crept up to the window in Bertel's car. Somehow he had obtained a fresh martini. He sat behind the wheel with much nobility. He turned his head, slowly and majestically, and stared at Tremble. Tremble, seeing this, planted a big kiss on Bertel's cheek and excused herself to go to the bathroom.

"Now pick out a nice desert that we might share," she said. "Something with chocolate."

Bertel looked eagerly at the menu and Tremble slipped out the door and jumped in the car with Ennui. They sped off. Tremble felt a little guilty over abandoning Bertel, but then she thought of the car and felt better.

The waiter appeared and presented the bill to Bertel. It was $7,819.69, plus appropriate tip of course. Bertel was dumbfounded. He reached for his wallet but it wasn't there. He looked up with wordless pleading. Several of the burlier waiters gathered around the table and tapped their heavy wooden pepper grinders on their meaty palms.

"I suppose he'll have to work it off, wouldn't you say?" one of them said. The rest of them nodded and chuckled in a most unpleasant manner.

Tremble likes
a house

"Oh look," said Ennui. "Bertel left his wallet in the car."

Tremble snatched it. "Let's see. Almost a thousand dollars, plus credit cards that haven't been cut up."

"It's a good thing that Bertel decided to finish without us," said Ennui. "Otherwise I'd have to sit in the back seat and it is soaked with gin. Bertel was driving like a madman. I was sloshing back and forth like a shirt in a washing machine. But I like my car. Don't you think I look good in it?"

"Oh Ennui," said Tremble. "We can drive around and drink and shop. Won't that be fun?"

Ennui smiled proudly. "Now where should we go? You know, I could really use a few more martinis to wash away the taste of that putrid wine."

But Tremble's attention had already wandered elsewhere. She discreetly fingered Intesti's card and then shoved it in her bra. Presently she began to moan and grab her stomach.

"I feel so full. Am I fat, Ennui?" she asked in a sad little voice.

"Your weight is perfect," said Ennui. "When I look

over and see your skinny legs, it reminds me of my days in school."

"You were in school, Ennui?"

"Of course I was in school. There was always a horrible smell of adolescent hormones in the air. Primitive. The only thing that made it tolerable was that I was drunk most of the time. Then there was this teacher who spanked me quite a bit—"

"Oh, Ennui, pull over somewhere, will you?" said Tremble.

"In this neighborhood? It's almost as bad as ours. You must be drunk on wine. I know I am. I'll have a horrible hangover tomorrow unless I get a martini very quickly."

"Quit being chatty. Just pull over somewhere, please."

"Absolutely not. Chef Intesti labored for hours on that meal. It was exquisite I am ashamed to admit. The dynamite-exploded pig salad was especially good today. The meal's perfection was marred only by the realization that Chef Intesti's greasiness is surpassed only by his greasiness. And then to watch him marinating your body with that lecherous salivating of his."

"Oh Ennui shut up! Oh just shut up and pull over. You're being an ass!"

"An ass am I? To protect you in this awful neighborhood? Well fine, then."

Ennui screeched the big Cadillac to a halt. "We'll stop

here and you go about and do your business. Right in front of this decrepit house. This neighborhood is so horrible. I've never enjoyed the aesthetics of poverty..."

Tremble had already bounded out the car and disappeared into the gaping French doors of an abandoned house, one of the thousands of century-old rotting wood carcasses spread throughout the city.

Ennui muttered and looked about him. "I need a martini in the worst way."

Ennui teaches
a child

Ennui fiddled with the radio and found the classical station. A young boy was strolling nearby and Ennui rolled down the window.

"You!" yelled Ennui. "Come here youngster."

The young boy approached slowly.

"Is there a bar nearby?"

The young boy silently pointed up the street.

"Well here, take this twenty." Ennui pulled the money out of Bertel's wallet. "Go get me a martini, extra dry. Gin of course. I imagine you people have plenty of gin in this neighborhood, though you will have to be dissuaded from mixing it with juice. Preferably Boodles, of course. Just order the most expensive one they'll make. There's a bonus on the way if the martini is extra cold and properly made. Now hurry along."

The Cadillac's window silently closed and Ennui once again basked in the silent aura of this temple to comfort. He found Gershwin on the radio and slid into pleasant, sleepy contemplation...

There was a tap at the window. The boy had returned with a martini.

Ennui motored the window down and took the martini. It was excellent—crisp, cold, dry and bracing. He handed over another twenty to the boy.

"Now don't loiter too far. I may need another one."

"But I have *homework*," said the boy.

Ennui sputtered over the mention of the word. "Nonsense. I never did homework. All I did in school was drink. And look at how I turned out—enjoying an excellent martini in a car worth a dozen of these houses. Let that be a lesson to you."

Ennui motored the window back up and tried to forget about the boy. "Silly youth. What is this world coming to," he muttered. He turned up the radio. The stereo system was excellent. He could hear all the instruments perfectly. He slipped into contemplation of Paris, of rain on sidewalks and glances in cafes...

Later, there was another rap on the window. Ennui shook himself awake and saw Tremble standing there, trying to get in. Ennui's martini glass was still in his hand, held upright, but it was empty, which was odd because it had been half-full when he fell asleep.

"I appear to have been sleep-drinking again," he told Tremble after she entered the car.

Tremble looked visibly refreshed and energized.

"Well, was it disgusting in there?" said Ennui. "Disgusting enough to match this disgusting practice of yours? You could have been raped, or killed, or forced to be in the presence of tacky furniture."

Tremble just smiled and sighed. "Actually it was quite nice. At first I thought the house was abandoned, but actually it was a crack house run by a proprietor with decent taste, though a little on the gaudy side."

"Oh no," groaned Ennui. "You smoked crack and are now hallucinating."

"Absolutely not," said Tremble. "I am much too drunk to smoke crack at the moment."

"Well, let's get out of here."

"We can't." Tremble looked at herself in the mirror and brushed her long hair. "I'm meeting someone."

"Someone you met in a crack house? Absolutely not."

Ennui locked the doors and revved the engine, preparing to speed off.

"Ennui!" cried Tremble. "If you leave I swear I will never marry you!"

Ennui turned off the engine. "You were going to marry me?"

"No of course not, silly. But if you left I would definitely not marry you."

"I get it. No, actually I don't get it."

"It's because you're drunk, Ennui. You'll understand in the morning."

"Okay," said Ennui. "But please don't tell me you're bringing a crack whore in the car."

"Of course not," said Tremble. "I met a nice gentleman, and I agreed to give him a lift."

"An old crack man I bet."

"I refuse to argue with you, Ennui. We'll just have to wait."

"Well in that case let's have a martini."

Ennui rolled down the window and ordered two martinis, extra dry of course.

They meet
an American
success story

Ennui and Tremble sipped their drinks in the car and waited. Presently they saw a man walk out of the house.

Ennui's face melted in horror. "Oh my gawd. It's worse than I thought. Quick, lock the doors!"

The man was about thirty. He was neatly dressed in a business suit and he carried a briefcase. He wore horn-rimmed glasses and had a conservative haircut. He walked gingerly to the car.

"You're bringing a lawyer into this car," cried Ennui. "Let's go let's go let's go!"

"Oh Ennui, quit with your dramatics. Lawyers make money," said Tremble. "Which is more than I can say about you. Now he is a nice young man and he is not attached right now. Be on your best behavior."

Ennui nodded, petrified. He gulped his martini.

The lawyer slid into the back seat. "Hello there," he said. He was a smiling, chipper thing. Tremble turned around and got on her knees and smiled over the headrest at him.

"Appreciate the ride," he said. "Name's Potts. James Potts. Some people call me Jack. It was a little joke my mom played on me. I'm a lawyer."

"Your mom sent you to law school as a joke?" said Ennui, appalled. "What a wicked woman."

"No, the name was a joke," Mr. Potts said.

"He's drunk," Tremble explained. "He's in no shape to do anything but keep his mouth shut and drive us."

"I see," Mr. Potts said. Then he looked around. "This is a nice car. Did you win it in a lawsuit? One of my clients used to drive a car like this—before he got bored and traded it in for a Rolls Royce. It was a very interesting American success story. Boy was he poor when I got him—smelled like an old mattress. He fell asleep—actually he passed out on a railroad track and the train came along and cut off his left small toe and what have you. Good god did we get some money out of that rail company. Good god we did! Ten million if I recall. He went on and moved up to Atlanta where I believe he became a motivational speaker and is very well respected in certain society circles. But I still think he likes to sip on the Boone's."

"How horrid," squealed Tremble.

"I'm afraid you're not the only one to have that reaction to my line of work," Mr. Potts sighed.

"Ennui, take note of this man," said Tremble. "You are bound to have some body part severed during one of your comatose drunken stupors and this man could have you properly compensated."

Ennui frowned and said, "What I would be pleased to know, Jack, is what you were doing coming out of a crack house?"

"Good question," said Mr. Potts. "I used to be like most people—I thought only prostitutes and mayors of major cities smoked crack. But though I had never seen crack, it was all I ever heard about. The insurance company lawyers would say you must be on crack, when I told them how much money I wanted. Then they would crack under the pressure once I got them in court. Clients always told me that the money they got was like crack. And I would get congratulated for cracking a case open. Everything good was compared to crack. I thought about that for a while, and then decided to find a crack house. I found this one, and so forth and so on."

Ennui yawned. "How blasé."

"Yes, I agree," said Tremble. "That seemed to be a ten dollar answer to a one dollar question."

The American Dream is explained

"Let's talk about something a bit more interesting," said Tremble. "But first, Ennui, order Mr. Potts a martini, as well as another one for you and me. It was very rude of you to not offer him one."

Ennui grunted in annoyance but motored down the window and placed his order.

"Now Mr. Potts, tell me, do ambulance chasers make a lot of money?" said Tremble.

"Oh yes," said the man. "Last year I made over thirty million, even though I graduated at the bottom of my law school class. No firm would take me, and I had mountains of debt, so I had to get busy."

Ennui yawned loudly.

"I'm sorry you don't think this is interesting," said Mr. Potts. "But would you be bored if I told you that I could get this young lady ten million within a month?"

"Yes I would be bored," said Ennui.

"Shut up Ennui," snapped Tremble. "Here we have an intelligent and enterprising man, a perfect success, and you carry on like such a child. Now suck on your martini and let Mr. Potts talk. Please, Mr. Potts, continue," said Tremble eagerly, her eyes widening.

"Well, it's very simple," said Mr. Potts. "You get a job at a large corporation—some place that is very dull—so dull that only men will work there. A bank or an engineering firm for example. We get you a job as a receptionist. Within a week the whole firm will know that a young girl has been hired. The executives will move you up to the top floor and make you an executive secretary."

"But I don't know how to type," said Tremble. "Come to think of it, I don't even know how to work."

"It doesn't matter," said Mr. Potts. "Most executives don't know how to work either. They just forward memos to each other and attend meetings. You'll get the hang of it."

"And what am I to do while you are working," said Ennui. "What about me?"

"Quit being selfish and shut up," said Tremble. "Please

continue, Mr. Potts."

"You would need to wear shorter skirts and tighter shirts. You may want to consider a push-up bra."

"I told you my breasts were small!" cried Tremble to Ennui.

Ennui was busy getting the martinis from the boy. "Oh enough with the breasts."

"In any case," said Mr. Potts. "It's only a matter of time before one of the executives puts a hand on you, and then we'll take a lot of money, and then some."

Tremble jumped up and down on her seat. "Oh James oh James oh James! I'm going to be a millionaire, finally."

"Yes, it's a sure thing," said Mr. Potts. "I've done it many times for many people. Come see me tomorrow and we'll work the whole thing out, and so on."

Suddenly, Mr. Potts' eyes averted and he looked at something out the window. "Not again," he said.

Business interrupts
the conversation

While the three were talking, a cloud covered the sun, darkening the street of shotgun houses. Then the sun broke through a crack in the clouds and went into their eyes.

"This sun is bound to warm my martini," said Ennui.

A man was standing at the end of the street. His pants swayed in the breeze and his teeth and jewelry glinted in the sun. He stood perfectly still, and his hands hovered near his hips.

"You should probably cover your ears," said Mr. Potts.

On the other end of the street, a man wearing a jacket with too much stuffing stepped out silently.

"Oh great, just great," said Ennui. "They've scared away my martini boy. What if I need a drink?"

"Don't worry, this happens all the time," Mr. Potts shot back. "Generally no one else gets killed."

Suddenly both men reached for their guns. The slower one was unfortunately riddled with dozens of bullets. The victor jumped into his white Lincoln and sped off.

"Goodness what a racket!" said Ennui.

"It looks like we have a new owner of the house," said Mr. Potts. "I hope he runs it as well as the old owner."

"The bathrooms *were* immaculate," said Tremble. "They were even better than at Intesti's. It would be a shame if they weren't kept up."

A siren was soon heard and Mr. Potts jumped out of the car.

"Excuse me for a minute," he said. "I have some work to do. It won't take long."

Mr. Potts ran out of the car and towards the bullet-ridden body. Meanwhile, an ambulance wheeled around the corner and ran over him.

"Oh my gawd!" cried Tremble.

Two men got out of the ambulance. One was skinny and stooped, with buck teeth. The other was short and round. He was eating a large roast beef po-boy that was dripping with gravy. The two leaned over and inspected the dead gangster.

"Is he dead?" called Tremble from the car.

"Him?" said the round one between bites. "Guess so. Anyway, if he weren't, what's the point of putting the plates on him? These drug dealers don't pay no taxes."

"No, the lawyer you just ran over."

"We just ran over a lawyer?" said the skinny one. "Well luckity ding-dang. I never believe that horoscope goop and today it came true!"

"Save him, save him!" shrieked Tremble.

The skinny one looked under the ambulance. "Nope, afraid his head's squished like that roach I had in my apartment last night. Dang that was a big roach. Hey Buttro," he called to the round one, "make that two body bags, and no need to super size it."

A bunch of police cars appeared out of nowhere. The policemen jumped out and immediately began drinking coffee and standing around. Some looked at the dead body of the gangster. Some of them looked under the ambulance at the corpse of James Potts. One of the cops reached down and touched the body of the gangster. He jumped back and shook his hand and did a little jig. "Oh goodness gracious, it's still warm," he exclaimed. "And would you take a look at his clothes! Fabulous I tell you, fabulous! There must be *something* you can do."

The skinny ambulance driver shrugged and pulled out the shock plates. "Maybe we'll try these. They hain't been working too well ever since I tried them on Buttro. I think he done blew them out. But what the diddly-doo."

The plates were applied to the gangster, and the body jumped several feet into the air.

"Dang that was high," said the skinny ambulance driver.

"Bet I can make it go higher," said the round one.

"Bet you cain't," said the skinny one.

Tremble was sniffling and wiping her nose with her arm. "Let's go," she said to Ennui. "All that money, gone."

Ennui tried to start the engine, but it just turned over a few times and then the battery went dead.

"How rude of Bertel to leave us with a dead battery," said Ennui. "I thought you said he was a friend of yours. I'd hate to walk home, or take a cab. I really don't like dealing with cabbies. Their cabs are always very dirty and they insist on speaking foreign languages. Mostly they hold you hostage by driving around in circles until you pay to get out. I never see the point in it. And my loafers are much too delicate to walk in."

Tremble pouted and finally said, "Darn you, aren't you good for anything?" She waved out the window. "Oh, yoo-hoo! You think we could borrow those shocky things for a moment?"

The day ends

Everyone stood around and the shock plates were applied to the Cadillac's engine. It worked like a charm. The engine jumped to life. Unfortunately, the radio exploded with a great shower of sparks and smoke. Afterwards, it would only play country music loudly, and Ennui was forced to toss James Potts' unfinished martini into it, which silenced it for the moment. Ennui was very upset because he could no longer listen to classical music. Also he was very drunk and on the verge of passing out.

They drove back home and Ennui promptly vomited off the front porch and passed out under a large azalea. Tremble went inside and fingered Chef Intesti's card and did various womanly things. She cried a little at the loss of the fortune James Potts was to bring her. But then she began to plan the next day. She fell asleep with Chef Intesti's card firmly between her fingers, fingers that were strong with the hope that springs eternal in the young.

IMPORTANT MATTERS

The landlord
pays a visit

Morning stretched its rosy fingers across the world, and even across Soraparu Street. The light shined on Ennui's young face, and the neighborhood came alive. Cars thumping with the acoustic power of small bombs prowled the street, and gunfire sounded in the air. A swarm of children on bicycles removed anything of value that wasn't bolted down. The old men took their places on their chairs, and the "crack" of those first fresh beers was heard as they were opened. Young merchants manned the street corners and began trading their wares.

And Tremble was awakened by a heavy thumping. Her landlord, Mr. Flatulus, had lumbered his flabby, bone-white body up on the porch, and pounded his hairy knuckles on the door. Rent had not been paid for seven months at 231 Soraparu Street, and well, that was just too long. Mr. Flatulus didn't want to evict Tremble and Ennui, for by all means they were model tenants. They hadn't burned the place down. They hadn't been incarcerated. And there hadn't been any multiple murders on the premises, as far as Mr. Flatulus knew, not that he wanted to.

Tremble heard the pounding and called out, "Oh, Ennui, quit trying to crush the ice, will you? I don't care if it makes a better martini."

But the pounding continued. Tremble groaned and slid out of bed. She foraged for clothing for a few minutes amongst the scattered piles, before finding a tablecloth that Ennui had stolen. She wrapped it around herself and made her way to the door.

"Ennui!" she yelled. "You know I need my beauty sleep!"

She opened the door to see Mr. Flatulus, wearing a tank top shirt and old shorts that had slid down to show the initial evidence of a canyon-like crack. He was breathing heavily, as he always seemed to do, and a stink hung in the air around him.

"Yes, Mr. Flatulus," said Tremble. She was hung over and cranky, and in no mood for this.

"Your rent! It's seven months past due!" cried Mr. Flatulus, jabbing his finger in the air for emphasis. He looked around nervously, for he never knew when one of his tenants might attempt a drive-by.

Normally, Tremble would furtively let her clothes slide open a little, to buy more time, but this morning she just rubbed her head, confused.

"I'm sure I sent Ennui to give you that rent five months ago," she said. "I remember it. It was just before Christmas, and Ennui had hired himself out as a Santa Claus. He was to distribute presents to a home of orphans. He was on his way to the orphanage with the presents, which were donated by some stupid charity. But he got drunk and never showed up. He sold the presents for food stamps. Then he took the food stamps and was about to go buy more liquor, but I made him sell the food stamps and told him to march straight to you with the money. I was very angry with him, you see."

These words swept past Mr. Flatulus without any effect. They breezed right by his sweaty body.

"Were you with him when he supposedly paid me?" sputtered Mr. Flatulus.

"Well, no, I wasn't," said Tremble. "I am much too busy to do those sorts of things."

"I must be paid," Mr. Flatulus burst out. "This is not public housing."

"It isn't?"

Mr. Flatulus smiled a greasy, devious smile. "Perhaps we could arrange some other sort of payment, eh?"

Tremble shivered in disgust. Once, in a moment of dire need, she had escaped six months rent by applying her hands to certain parts of his body. But she felt so disgusted afterwards that she went on a drinking binge that lasted several months, during which all sorts of alarming activities occurred. Never again. The very sight of this bloated worm made her want to vomit. She promised payment by the next day and slammed the door. There would be plenty of money in Bertel's wallet. If not, the wheels from Bertel's car could easily raise the necessary sum.

She turned around and looked at her apartment. Laundry undone for months. Broken furniture where Ennui had collapsed and shattered coffee tables, side tables, lamps and anything else that could be collapsed upon. Pile upon pile of empty gin bottles. Martini glasses scattered and unwashed. Lamps, tablecloths, silverware, curtains, plates and anything else that could be stolen from restaurants and bars. Dozens of issues of *Vanity Fair* were strewn everywhere. Tremble sighed and felt the card in her hand. And then she frowned.

Ennui wakes
a changed man

Ennui finally awoke when an empty gin bottle hit his head. He was still lying under the azalea bush.

"Ouch," said Ennui. "What was that?"

"The same thing that put you to sleep," said Tremble.

"Oh," said Ennui. "What are you doing?"

"I'm cleaning." Tremble was throwing broken furniture and trash and bales of clothing off the front porch. A large crowd of neighbors had gathered and there was a feeding frenzy occurring. The majority of items were grabbed before they could hit the ground.

"Our apartment needs cleaning?" said Ennui. "Why aren't we having a maid do this?"

"Shut up Ennui," said Tremble. "And it's not our apartment. It's my apartment. I'm graciously letting you stay here after you burned down your last apartment."

Ennui scratched his head. "Oh, yes, that was a good party. I had no idea that the building wasn't more fire resistant. How was I to know that trash fires were meant to be outdoors? There should have been some sort of warning label somewhere. I really should sue. What's the name of that friend of yours? Potts something or other. Oh, that's right, he's dead."

Tremble groaned and grabbed her hair. She was having one of those moments. "Oh, Ennui," she cried, stomping her foot. Then she looked down at him. "By the way, what is that awful striped outfit you are wearing?"

Ennui looked at his clothing and sat up. "It appears to be a prison uniform."

Tremble leaned close to examine it. On the front was the number "3822", and on the back "Angola State Pen". Tremble held her nose. "And what is that disgusting smell on your breath? It smells like, like malt liquor," she said with a shiver.

Ennui looked around. He picked up a large bottle. "Yes, here's the empty. It appears I have been sleep-drinking malt liquor."

"Enough of your antics. Just give me Bertel's wallet so I can pay the rent."

"It appears to be gone," said Ennui.

"Well then where is the car? We're going to have to sell some part of it."

"It was over there." Ennui rubbed his head in thought. "It seems to have disappeared along with my smoking jacket, my French cuff shirt with my cuff links, my slacks and my tasseled loafers. And my martini glass is gone. I believe I had a fresh one right before I vomited and passed out. It looks as though I was sent to prison last night for some crime that I cannot remember, after which I escaped and made it here. I appear to have celebrated my escape by drinking this large bottle of malt liquor. I must have developed a taste for the stuff when I was doing time."

"You idiot!" shrieked Tremble. "Obviously an escaped convict stole Bertel's wallet, his Cadillac, your clothing and your martini glass, and left you with this disgusting get-up. And now he is enjoying the life which properly belongs to me!"

"Or, yes, that could be the case," said Ennui. "But it

seems a bit far fetched. Now how can I get back my clothes? I believe I must break back into prison. Very dangerous I'm guessing. I don't think there's ever been a case of anyone breaking into Angola."

"Oh, just shut up! How are we to pay rent?"

"Can't you go on another date with Mr. Flatulus?"

Tremble groaned viciously. "I'll go on a date you numskull. I'm going to call up Chef Intesti and marry him."

"I see—you're going to marry Chef Intesti because I no longer have my smoking jacket and cuff links? How shallow of you."

Tremble grabbed at her hair and screamed and marched inside and closed the door. Ennui sauntered up the stairs and knocked gently.

"Go away Ennui," said Tremble.

"Can't I mix our morning martinis?"

"We're out of gin. Go away."

"But where am I to go?"

"I don't care. Go to prison, or to hell, whichever you prefer. Just never come back here."

"But I have no money to buy a martini. And I would be very embarrassed walking into a respectable establishment in my prison uniform."

There was no sound in return. Ennui jiggled the door. It was locked. He sat on the porch for a long time. The sun shone hotter. The crickets began to sing.

Ennui stared at the men on the porches, and they stared at him. He got up and walked away, wondering when his next drink would appear.

Tremble
straightens up

A young lady answered when Tremble called the number on Chef Intesti's card.

"Yes," said the lady.

"Is this the number of Chef Intesti?" asked Tremble, with a childlike nervousness.

"Where did you get this number?" said the lady. It was a professional voice, young and controlled, with northern efficiency.

"Chef Intesti gave me his card."

"What color is the card?" asked the lady.

"What?"

"I said what color is the card," said the lady, more rudely this time.

"Why, it's green."

There was a pause on the phone. "Well, why didn't you say so?" The lady suddenly turned very friendly. "Sorry to get testy, but if you only knew what kinds of calls I have to put up with. It is so nice to have someone who actually got a green card. So when are you available?"

"Pardon?"

"When are you available to sleep with Chef Intesti?"

"I didn't know I was sleeping with Chef Intesti," said Tremble.

"Of course you are my dear girl. I mean you will. Every one of you ends up sleeping with Chef Intesti."

"Perhaps I am not what you think," Tremble snapped.

"Then who are you? You got the green card, so you must be a green card girl. Otherwise, hang up. Go ahead—I'm waiting. See. You're still on the line. There there, my dear. Now be a good girl and tell me when you are free."

"I'll have to check my calendar."

"Don't bother my darling honey. I always forget that your type will be available whenever Chef Intesti has an opening. So let's forget the charade, shall we? I see that the Chef has an opening on Thursday—no that appears to be taken by a fund raiser to save an orphanage. It is on the brink of bankruptcy, and several of the children drowned themselves in the river after Santa didn't bring them anything for Christmas last year. Chef Intesti is so kind to cook for the fundraising dinner. Otherwise those vicious little brats will be housed at the nearest prison when the orphanage goes under. But I suppose it's where they'll end up eventually. And you do have a green card, and the

Chef is so busy. Let's just set it then. Nine o'clock. Chef Intesti's limousine will pick you up. Now what is your address?"

Tremble gave it to her.

"Now look spiffy—Chef Intesti doesn't like sagging melons or limp celery," said the lady before hanging up.

Tremble hung up the phone and there was empty, lonely silence in the apartment. She had no radio or television to turn on, for they had been stolen by neighbors or sold by Ennui for liquor. She didn't realize how much Ennui's chatter filled up the apartment. And she really needed a martini.

She began to clean, and to scrub, and to wash. She went through layer upon layer of clothing and trash and dirt. Memories shook free like dust. Parents and siblings and aunts and lots of uncles. Boyfriends coming and going. Then the drinking Ennui, arriving on campus after an extended stay in Europe, where he had been banned from several countries for vague reasons—something having do to with a scheme to illegally smuggle the French into rural China. Ennui prowling the curvy hidden streets on campus in his long car, and finding her, then the blurry years, and then this.

After she had cleaned, the house looked empty. There was little but a few sticks of furniture that were too heavy to pawn or steal, and bare plaster walls covered with marks and scratches. She was tired, and there was a day and a half until her date with Intesti. She locked the doors and windows and closed all the curtains. She drank a large glass of water, put plugs in her ears, and got under the sheets. Her dreams were strange and stupid and made no sense.

Conversation
releases
the winds of love

The long black limousine crept over the street, silently and slowly, like night overtaking the day.

"Driver, you sure we in the right block," asked the esteemed, wealthy and world-famous Chef.

"Yes sir," said the driver with authority.

"Ugh! This neighborhood stinkin like rottin veggies. Look at these poor people. How can they live like this. Can't they be rich?"

"It *is* a shame, sir."

"I wonders if I gots the right broad. Great piece of ass but dumb as a stick. I was thinkin she might be from Hollywood. But now this pit. Crap this place sucks."

"Pardon my asking, but was she alone, sir?"

"Nah. Some butthead was there too. Tried to mix it up with a couple of my waiters. The wine steward went quittin on me after that. But it don't matter. There's only so much yappin you can do on wine before you gotta drink the crap. Then some loaf walks into my joint and tries to jump the check. My waiters work him over pretty good. Everybody gotta pay the Chef. We put him to work scrubbin dishes. He's a real animal with those dishes, you know."

There was some silence as the car bounded slowly over the potholes and past the houses of the fading city.

"Yeah, so many broads," said Chef Intesti philosophically. "That's the curse from being famous like myself. Yeah, I know whatchu thinkin. You see, this is how it are. For the average guy, chicks is like water. He needin them to survive. Birthin the kids. But there ain't no flavor to it."

"Very interesting, sir," said the driver.

"But you takes somebody like me here. To me, babes is like wine. You open it, drink it, then throw it out. Wine goes to crap after it gets open, you know."

"You could always drink water, sir."

The great Chef grunted in disapproval. "Tough for you to understand." There was some silence, then, "Hey, you is new, ain't you?"

"Yes sir."

"Then why don't I know who you is?"

"Because I'm new, sir."

"Yeah yeah. Guess that makes sense." Another pause from the Chef, then, "Crap this car smells like gin."

"Here we are," said the driver abruptly. He pulled up to Tremble's house.

An urban entrepreneur approached the limousine. The driver took the liberty to lower Chef Intesti's window. That is the mark of a good servant, to anticipate the master's needs, thought the driver.

Chef Intesti tried to shrink away, but the driver lowered all the windows. "What is you doin?" shrieked the Chef.

"Let's see here," said the urban entrepreneur. "We have a special tonight, buy two rocks, get one free. Also we are pleased to announce that we now accept all major credit cards. But please, no personal checks. May I take your order, sir?"

"I ain't no customer of yours!"

"Well then, I'd like to invite you to purchase our frequent buyer discount card."

"Good god rolls up this window!"

Tremble came bounding down the steps and into the street. "Shoo shoo. Shoo away from here little fly. Don't bother his beautiful limousine."

The urban entrepreneur slunk away. "He was in a limo," he said by way of explanation.

"Shoo away little fly," said Tremble.

"Allow me to open your door," said the driver.

Tremble didn't look at the servant—she seldom looked at the lower classes—but she smelled a certain smell. It was a smell of gin and dry vermouth. She looked up.

"Ennui," she hissed. "How dare you."

"Please watch your step, miss," said Ennui.

"What are you doing here?"

"Earning a living ma'am, the god given right of every American. Need to pay rent, ma'am," said Ennui. He was dressed in a black suit and black cap.

"You ruin my chances with Intesti and I'll castrate you."

"Let me help you inside." Ennui kicked Tremble in the rear, propelling her into the car, and shut the door. Then he got in and roared off.

Tremble landed in Intesti's arms. Her little black dress was up around her ears, displaying her underwear. She tried to pull her dress down but Ennui was driving at great speeds, bumping and bounding over the pothole-filled roads, and taking turns on the narrow streets with race-car like precision. Both Tremble and Chef Intesti were thrown back and forth and up and around.

"Driver!" screamed Chef Intesti. "Hey slow this rig down!"

"I would gladly slow down, if you care to be beaten to death and your beautiful date violated. Kindly look behind you," sniffed Ennui.

There was a car made of Bondo and tinted windows in close pursuit. It had one headlight on and was belching great plumes of smoke.

"You see," called out Ennui over the ruckus. "This limousine is like a great carcass of wealth. You are bound to pick up some flies if you drag it through a neighborhood such as this. Not to worry, though. They seldom have enough gas in them to make it too far. And from the look of things, he is burning quite a bit of oil as well. Yes, there he goes. He's gone now. It is the economic principal of diminishing returns, of course."

Ennui slowed the limousine to a relaxing speed, and the lovebirds in the rear were able to compose themselves. Chef Intesti's eyes brushed Tremble's body with an approving sauce. She was wearing the little black dress and had her hair up. She looked quite the sophisticate.

They drove slowly along one of the avenues of obsolete mansions. Tremble stared lovingly at all the grandness around her.

"Champagne," belched the Chef.

"Certainly," said Ennui. "But be sure the bottle is chilled and freshly opened. There is nothing worse than flat, warm champagne."

"Not you," yelled the Chef. He closed the privacy screen. "That driver gettin fired tomorrow," he said to

Tremble.

"That's good," she replied.

Now the Chef was alone with his dish. He poured two glasses of champagne. There was that uncomfortable period of silence that occurs during dates before the couple gets drunk.

"Thimble, what's your story?" said the Chef.

"It's Tremble," said Tremble, between gulps of champagne.

"Yeah whatever. So spill it."

Tremble took a deep breath and exhaled a rambling tale about how she was raised on a farm in Kansas and lived an idyllic life with her two loving parents. Then a tornado came and picked up the house with her two parents in it. She never saw them again. Fortunately, a band of gypsies was passing through, and they saved her. In the band was a kindly old Indian woman who just happened to be a master in the pleasuring arts. This woman took Tremble under her wing, and before she passed away her secrets were handed down. Tremble said she had only fully unleashed this art on a man once, and it sent him into a vegetable-like state from which he refused to leave. She thought he was still living in Philadelphia, but believed he was back to normal now. After she reached adulthood, the gypsies sent her to college by cashing a zero-coupon bond they had purchased for her during childhood. She attended college for several years, but left in order to live among the poor in simple conditions so that she could practice charity, which was her love, and chastity, free from the temptations of wealthy, good-looking men.

Chef Intesti leaned to one side and let loose a terrific fart, and he decided that he must de-bone this hot little chicken at once.

Tremble
wants to see
Intesti's

Tremble and the Chef rode around for a little while in the limousine. Apparently the Chef thought that he would be able to bed her in transit after a few glasses of champagne.

The Chef droned on about his various accomplishments, and listed the famous celebrities he had fed, and how high his stock price was, and how successful his restaurants were, and his cookbooks and cooking shows and so forth. Tremble saw where this was going, and was not about to let it happen in a limousine, of all places, especially from the man she was going to marry. That just wouldn't do.

She mentally listed and summarized the various

instructional articles in women's magazines about how to wed a man. She seemed to remember that the first step was to show interest in his conversation. The next step was to show interest in his work.

"Weren't you going to show me your kitchen?" she asked.

"My kitchen?" said the Chef. "Nah, is a dull place. Nothin but work. You wouldn't be interested."

"Oh yes, I really, really would be," said Tremble.

"Gets hot," said the Chef.

"But I love hot places," said Tremble.

"Gets dirty," said the Chef. "Messy."

"I love hot and dirty and messy."

Intesti considered what it would be like under the heat lamps. He lowered the privacy screen. "Driver, you betta be pointin this rig at my restaurant."

Much to the Chef's surprise, no driver was to be seen, despite the fact that the car was careening along at a high rate of speed.

"Driver!" called the Chef.

Ennui's head popped up and his hands went back on the steering wheel. "Yes sir."

"Where the crap was you?" said the Chef.

"Right here, sir," said Ennui.

"Nah you wasn't."

"Then where was I?"

"That's what I'm askin," said the Chef, flustered.

"What exactly were you asking?"

"Where you was?"

"Right here," said Ennui.

"Ah forget about it," said the Chef. "Crap I smell gin."

"I'm sorry that I can't afford to wear a designer cologne," sniffed Ennui, "but that doesn't give you the right to insult it."

"Just drive me to my restaurant," said the Chef.

"You own a restaurant?"

"I own seven joints! And I is gettin one put in at Orlando next week."

"Pardon me," Ennui interrupted. "If we're going to Orlando, you're going to have to come up with some gas money, sir. And I believe that would qualify for overtime pay."

"Nah, you numbnuts, I want to go to my restaurant here."

"You have a restaurant here?"

"Yeah. Go to it."

"Which restaurant is it?"

"Intesti's, you ass-wipe."

"Intesti's? I've never heard of it."

"It be the most famous joint in the town!" the Chef howled.

"Excuse me sir," said Ennui, "I may be just a lowly

employee, but I deserve the same amount of respect that any man deserves. Please don't abuse me just because no one knows where your restaurant is. I consider that quite arrogant, cruel and unfair. How is it my fault that your restaurant isn't better known? Perhaps with some proper marketing this problem could be rectified."

The Chef groaned. Tremble slapped Ennui on the side of the head. "Corner of Race and Annunciation," she said. "Don't be such an idiot."

"Oh, that restaurant," said Ennui. "Why I'm glad to be in your employ, sir, in order to have the opportunity to tell you what a vomitous meal I had there recently. My hamburger was completely overcooked, and my french fries were cold and had the texture of congealed grease."

"My place don't be servin burgers," said the Chef. "You confusin me with some other chef."

"I didn't order a hamburger," said Ennui, "But that was all the kitchen could produce. Quite poor, actually. And all those awful rumors about no dog, cat or rat being safe—"

Tremble raised the privacy screen. "We will have to fire that driver," she said.

"We?" said the Chef.

Tremble and Ennui
see
an old friend

They pulled up to Intesti's and a valet hurled himself at the car and opened the door. Chef Intesti escorted his date through the door and into the crowded restaurant, strutting like a rooster. He was wearing a black suit with a banded-collar shirt that allowed a bouquet of chest hairs to poke through.

Ennui motored down the window. The valet approached.

"Who's he got this time," said the valet, a young, fit man from a small, clean town.

"I don't know, some broad," said Ennui. "She wanted to see the kitchen."

"Yeah, they all do," said the valet. "But who knows what goes on back there. He doesn't show it to many people."

"But he's showing it to her."

"Hell, if I had a date with her I'd show her everything I had."

"Not if I were Intesti," said Ennui. "He's got the smallest cock in the city."

"That so?" said the valet, nodding thoughtfully.

"It's just what I've heard," said Ennui.

Ennui drove to the other side of the street and double parked. He needed a martini in the worst way, so he went into Intesti's. It was packed. He pushed his way through the crowd to the front of the bar. Then he felt a slap on the back of his head.

"Ouch," said Ennui.

"How dare you interfere with my date like this," said Tremble. She was at the bar sipping a martini. "And how did you manage to get this job?"

"Prison to work program," said Ennui. "I actually had several lucrative job offers through this charity, including a bank executive and a political appointee, but I sacrificed and took this job in order to save you from a horrible fate. Did you see how his hair was sticking out of his shirt?"

"Oh, Ennui, just don't interfere. You make him so angry."

"Did you miss me?"

"Just shut up."

"I need a martini."

"I need food," said Tremble, looking about. "It's been days."

Ennui followed her glance. "Where's the Chef?" he asked. "Playing with his tool?"

Tremble pointed. The Chef was being mobbed by hundreds of adoring diners who were cooing over the superbness of his food. In fact, the whole restaurant was in a state of heightened excitement. Couples argued with feverish intensity: "No my dish is better—no *my* dish is better dear, just ask the Chef!"

"He is dull as dishwater," said Tremble. "Oh, and please refrain from napping while you drive us. It's very dangerous."

"Why, Tremble," said Ennui, "I'm afraid you aren't your old self. Where's my Tremble of yesteryear? You are becoming positively matronly."

Tremble sighed. "I don't know, Ennui. I just don't know."

"Perhaps we should get you some food. A little perk-me-up?"

They snuck through the kitchen doors. The employees didn't notice them, as they all seemed to be in hushed conversations about the Chef. "I hear it is this short," said one. "About the size of a baby carrot," said another.

"Isn't it just awful how these rumors get started," said Ennui.

Tremble was busy ladling soup into her mouth from an open pot. "Mmmmf," she moaned in pleasure.

"Come along, now," said Ennui. "There will be plenty of treats to sample."

The kitchen was fairly typical of most trendy restaurants. There was the usual equipment—stoves cooking, grills searing, heat lamps heating, machine guns tenderizing meat, and so forth.

And waiters ran into the kitchen and yelled at the cooks:

"Where's my pan-seared, car-killed fragrant meat?"

The cooks yelled back:

"The ticket was for a gas-killed, not car-killed fragrant meat!"

Then they would yell and curse each other, and each other's mothers, and each other's ancestors. Then the cook would finally give the waiter the dish, but only after heating the plate to scorching temperatures.

"Aaaaheeee!" screamed the waiter as he hustled out the door, his hand smoking.

Something caught Tremble's eye. "Look at that big ape thing over there," she said.

They looked over at the dish-washing station, where an ape-like man was chained by the leg to an enormous sink. He wore no shirt and hair covered his body.

"Ungha ungha," said the ape man.

"It appears to be your friend, Bertel," said Ennui.

The ape man saw them and began to jump up and down.

"Oh, Bertel darling, it's good to see you too," Tremble called out.

"Ungha ungha ungha," said the ape man. He got on his

knees and began to plead.

"Oh, I'm fine, thanks for asking. Be sure to give me a call when you are finished here. We'll do lunch. Ta ta!"

"Imagine trying to walk out of here without paying your bill," Ennui sniffed. "It's positively absurd."

Tremble then clutched her stomach. "Oh I shouldn't have eaten that soup. I feel fat already. Do I look fat?"

Before Ennui could say anything, Tremble had slipped through a door.

The Chef
practices
his art

Ennui followed Tremble into a dark hall.

"This doesn't look like a bathroom," said Tremble. "It must be around here somewhere."

"Shhh!" said Ennui. "I hear something. It sounds like animals."

They listened, and sure enough there was the sound of grunting, and then a high-pitched squeal, followed by a long groan and finally a slopping noise like a large animal wallowing in mud.

"They must be keeping the wild beasts in here for slaughter," said Ennui. "I doubt this disgusting habit of yours is worth being trampled underfoot. I could spill my martini!"

"Oh shut up Ennui," said Tremble. "It's not animals."

She strode up to a door at the end of the hall and cracked it open. It was the Chef's office. Inside, with all his energy, the great Chef was teaching a young fan how to make a dessert.

"Say it, say it!" howled the Chef. "We is makin a banana split!"

"Split me with your banana!" said the girl.

"I splittin you with my banana! I SPLITTIN YOU WITH MY BANANA!"

Then there was a gurgling, hissing sound. The Chef had pulled out a large can of whipped cream and was spraying it profusely.

"I'm shocked he'd be using store bought, not made from scratch," Tremble whispered.

Then the phone in the Chef's office rang loudly.

"Crap," said the Chef. He got up, leaving the girl with an annoyed look on her face. "It be my marketin department in New York."

He picked up the phone. "Now what?... A breakthrough?... It better be good.... Yeah, yeah, road kill dishes?... Keep talkin.... You think people will go for it?... Call it air aged and tire tenderizin?... Yeah maybe.... Not sure people is that stupider—hey listen to me what am I sayin?... Somethin else?... Yeah, what, I'm busy here.... A bone?... No crappin way.... Brushed with an air sauce and stewed in water?... You tested in Vegas and it sellin?... Yeah you right, no fat.... Think of the margin on that damn bone!... Okay roll it out national."

The Chef hung up and chuckled to himself.

The girl crossed her arms. "I thought you were a great Chef," she said.

Here the Chef let out a great peal of laughter, causing his hairy flesh to visibly shake. When he stopped, he slipped his arm around the girl. "Look missy. Who needs to know about cookin when for ten bucks an hour I hire losers from culinary school."

She still wasn't convinced.

"I gots money baby, lots of money!" said the Chef.

That made her feel a little better.

"And I is celebrity! Hell, I be a real do-gooder. If there ain't no celebrity chefs, the rich would be starvin to death. They only eat celebrity chef food!"

At this the girl seemed convinced that there was some worth in the Chef. "I guess you're right," she mumbled.

"Now," said the Chef. "How about a salad? A tossed salad. Where be that oil vat I had sittin around."

Tremble pulled herself away from the door and closed it.

"Don't you want to see how your husband-to-be makes a salad," said Ennui.

"Don't be a turd," said Tremble. She walked with some purpose down the hall. "All men do that before they get married."

With that, Tremble and Ennui each felt a strong little hand grabbing them. It was a smart-looking young woman in a business suit.

"Oh thank god there you are," she breathed out in relief. "Thank god! The Chef has been worried sick about you. He thought that you had been trampled in the rush of people. Now let's just bring you outside and figure out what to tell the Chef. Somehow he lost you with all the people crowding around him. They just love him so. Imagine, losing a green card girl. It would be a disaster for my career. Now be a good girl and don't ever tell anyone, and especially not the Chef that you were back here."

She hustled them out the back through a door, up an alley and out into the street. She looked Ennui over. "You must be the Chef's driver. You should go back to your limo and pretend you've been polishing it the whole time. The Chef hates to see idleness. Idle hands are the devil's tools, or something like that, you know."

A small group of the Chef's handlers appeared from nowhere.

"Got her?" said one.

"Yes!" said the young woman, making her hand into a fist and pumping it.

"Whew," said several in the crowd. "It was a green card girl. What a close call. We should just say she was out here breathing fresh air."

"That's right," said another. "She's been out here the whole time."

"Breathing fresh air," said yet another.

Ennui, seeing that this meeting might go on for some time, went inside and came out with a large martini.

Tremble looked bored. "This hasn't been much of a date so far," she said. "All I've done is watch the Chef pay attention to his fans."

The Chef's entourage immediately jumped to defend him.

"That's what it's like to be with a famous person," said one.

"Chef Intesti is very famous you know," said another.

A new suit ran up to the group and quickly proclaimed, "We have a situation. We have to get the Chef out here now! I just got a call from the police. The orphans are rioting."

"What? How dare they," said the young woman. "Don't they keep those brats chained down?"

"The orphans haven't been fed in days and were told they would be fed tonight by the Chef!"

A few other handlers came out, dragging the Chef so fast that some of his clothes had apparently fallen off.

Just then an enormous mob of children rounded the corner and headed in the Chef's direction. They were yelling unprintable things. The Chef's entourage quickly tossed the Chef, his clothes, and Tremble into the limousine and it sped away. Several children were hanging on but Ennui's driving caused them to fall off.

"Good doin," wheezed the Chef. "Shook those kids right off the hood."

"What?" said Ennui. "There were children on the hood?"

Love arises
from
pleasurable driving

It was decided by the Chef that they should attend a small but exclusive party being held by some of the Chef's friends down in the old French district. There were bound to be artists, society ladies, writers, and other annoying people in the group. Chef Intesti loved to bring his young vixens to these gatherings. And he liked to be remonstrated by the older women. "Oh, Chef," they would say. "She's practically a baby. *You little devil*."

Ennui drove up the avenues that he had gotten to know over the past few years. He balanced his martini in one hand and hung his other out of the window. He liked the warm breeze in his hair. He could smell the mixture of mustiness and lust from the gnarled oaks and flowers crowding the roads.

The privacy screen was up, so he didn't know what was being transacted behind him, except he could detect a slight movement.

Then he heard something horrible—it made his stomach churn. It was terrible enough to make spies tell their secrets and hostage takers run screaming from their buildings. It was the dull, awful twang of country music.

Where had he heard this? Then he saw—just ahead of him—the Cadillac. "My smoking jacket!" cried Ennui.

He followed the car. And the car picked up speed. Ennui pressed the accelerator. They whizzed through red lights, just inches away from being killed by crossing traffic. They jumped railroad tracks. They screeched and wheeled through the old wharves and warehouses on the river. They shot down the narrow roads, slid across the levees, and came within inches of crashing through the cypress trees into the great muddy river. And then, suddenly, the Cadillac gently pulled up in front of an old townhouse in the French district.

Ennui looked at the address. It was the very same place he had been instructed to take the Chef and Tremble. He sat in the limousine and watched a swarthy young man climb out of the Cadillac with great dignity. The man held a martini in one hand, and the light from a gas street lamp glinted off one of his cuff links. He wore a smoking jacket, tasseled loafers, and elegant slacks. The man gingerly bounded up the three marble steps to the townhouse, knocked, and went in.

Ennui got out with some irritation and opened the passenger door. Tremble and the Chef tumbled out, smoking cigarettes.

"A pleasant drive I hope," said Ennui.

"We drivin?" said the Chef. "Yeah I guess we was drivin."

"Are we still parked outside of the restaurant?" asked Tremble.

"No, we're in front of the party," Ennui snapped.

"Let's get our asses in there," said the Chef.

Tremble and the Chef got up and went towards the building. "A bit flushed, are we?" said Ennui.

"It's just my rouge, silly driver," said Tremble.

Tremble and the Chef went inside. Ennui fumed. Tremble and his clothes were inside. And here he was in a stupid black cap and suit, standing outside of someone's limousine. This wasn't the position the son of an industrialist should be in. He walked down the antiquated street of tall doors and crooked buildings, looking for a bar.

Ennui escapes
his problems
at a bar

Ennui had trouble finding a bar to his liking. At one bar there was an open-mike poetry reading.

"Vomitous," Ennui sniffed.

At the next bar there was a brass band playing and a group of tourists jumping up and down while pick-pockets extracted their wallets. "Being robbed once in a week is enough for me," Ennui snorted.

Finally he found a very small bar with a little red door. There was a sign on the door that said:

IF THERE'S A FLY IN YOUR DRINK
IT'S ON THE HOUSE

And below it was another sign that said:

NO SHIRT, NO SHOES

After Ennui reviewed the signs, he pulled the door open and ducked in. The place was dark and contained a long wooden bar. Decades of smoke and liquor had aged everything in the bar to a deep brown patina, including the patrons, who consisted of old men who had been sitting on the same stools for so long that it was difficult to tell the beginning from the end.

Ennui ordered a martini.

"A martini?" cackled the barmaid. "Hey guys, hear this, he wants a martini!"

The men all laughed and slapped each other's backs and yelled out "martini!" at various intervals.

"Well that's what he's going to get, then," said the barmaid matter-of-factly. The men shut up and went back to their beers.

The barmaid was a crusty old thing. She poured Ennui a martini. It was excellent. However, a fly immediately dove into the drink and died.

"Ma'am, I believe there's a fly in my drink," said Ennui politely.

"It's on the house, honey," said the barmaid.

"Thank you," said Ennui.

"That'll be five dollars."

"Your sign says it's on the house if there's a fly in it."

"Yeah, the fly's on the house."

"Oh," said Ennui. He handed over some money. "By the way, what's the name of this place?"

"No name anymore," said the barmaid.

"It doesn't have a name?"

"I forgot it when I was young."

"Why don't you give it a name?"

"Because then it would be the wrong name. What if I remembered the right name?" she said. "Hey guys, he wants to know what the name of this place is!"

All the men cackled and slapped each other's backs but none of them could remember the name of the bar.

One of the patrons scooted close to Ennui. It was an old man drinking a Falstaff. He wore a cap that said:

IF YOU CAN READ THIS, YOU NEED NEW GLASSES

"What's your problem, mack," said the man.

"My problem, sir?" said Ennui.

"Everyone in here's got a problem."

"Okay I'll tell you," said Ennui, who then proceeded to tell the man his life story, up to the point of seeing Tremble go into a house with a greasy chef.

"Oh," said the man. "My first wife sounds exactly like this woman, Pimple."

"Tremble," said Ennui.

"Whatever. Before I married her she had run through all her money. Then once she ran through my money, she didn't want me anymore. She ran around chasing rich men. I was depressed and I went into a bar. And in the bar I happened to be talking to an old man who told me exactly how to get a woman like this to worship you, money or no money. All I had to do was buy him a beer, and he told me the secret. And it worked."

"And what was the secret?" asked Ennui.

"Buy me a beer and I'll tell you," said the man.

Ennui bought a beer, which the man grabbed and swallowed rapidly. Then the man began to sway a little and he threw up on himself and passed out.

"Darn, I was about to learn that secret," said Ennui.

Another old man got up and sat next to Ennui. He handed Ennui a flyer. The flyer had a picture of an old man on it, and it said "MISSING" in large letters at the top. Under the picture was a description of the man, the circumstances under which he had disappeared, and a number to call if he was spotted.

Ennui looked at the picture, then at the man. "That's you in the picture," said Ennui.

"That's right," said the man. "I'm missing. Have been for years. Have you seen me?"

"I'm looking at you right now. Whose number is this on the flyer," said Ennui.

"That's my number," said the man.

"Is there a reward for finding you?"

"Nope," said the man.

"Well, then why should I report that I have located you?"

"That's what I keep telling myself, that I need to offer a reward."

"I'm afraid I can't help you," said Ennui, with a touch of indignation. "I can't be running around hunting down missing persons for nothing. I do believe there is a government bureau that spends my tax dollars performing that function."

The man looked dejected. "Yes, I've tried them, but they weren't much help. Bureaucracy, you know." He slunk off into the darkness.

Ennui finished his martini and got off the stool. Sitting there wasn't going to help things.

"Hey, aren't you going to give me a tip," said the barmaid.

"Oh yes, how rude of me. Short the stock of Intesti's Restaurants, Inc.," said Ennui.

"Come again," said the barmaid, who went back to pouring beers.

A Grande Madame's largesse is experienced

Meanwhile, Chef Intesti had escorted Tremble into the home of Madame Pusillanious. The Madame was a very large woman who lived in a very old townhouse.

The townhouse was in the city's French district, an area where Madame had lived for some time. She had married twice, and both husbands had fled, after which she had extracted sizable amounts of money from them.

Although originally from Milwaukee, she went by the name Madame, for like most residents of the French district, she had pretensions to royalty. At one time she had paid a genealogist to look into her roots. After tens of thousands of dollars, the best he could come up with was that in the 1700s, a French peasant with a similar name had fallen down drunk under the carriage of a marquis. The peasant had died a messy death. This was enough for Madame to claim blood relations to French aristocracy.

Like many residents of the old French district, Madame had attached a conspicuous plaque to her house, designating it a historic landmark, due to the fact that the house was older than houses that had been built more recently. There were always tourists stopping to read this plaque, and Madame Pusillanious took great pleasure in the attention, feeling as though her house was a royal residence visited by commoners.

This grandest of ladies had also renamed her residence "House of Pusillanious" because she had lived there for seven years, despite the place having been built in the 1820s and housing dozens of owners over the years.

Madame did her best to fashion the house into a salon

for intellectuals and artists. As a result, there were always annoying and pretentious people gathering in the house at night, drinking and enjoying the company of Madame Pusillanious.

Madame was having one of these gatherings when the renowned Chef Intesti entered with his beautiful date. They had joined what was turning out to be a glittering collection of personalities. In the crowd was a noted preservationist who still lived in an original 1700s Creole cottage without electricity or running water. The other guests would not sit near him. Also present was a prominent author who wrote books about himself and sold them as novels. There was a famous artist who specialized in painting canvasses white. Sitting next to the great Madame was an interior decorator to whom all the wealthy women were paying morbidly large amounts to redecorate their houses. And of course there was Madame Pusillanious herself, wearing a white gown with enough frills, laces and bows to dress a dozen brides. On her head was a large hat that had several bushels of flowers sticking out of it.

At the time, Madame was being entertained by her dog, Poopsie, in front of the group. "Mama loves her little Poopsie, doesn't she?" Madame squealed. The little white dog jumped up and down and yipped. "Yeeees, mama loves her little *Poopsie poo*. Mama loves to play with her

Poopsie. Mama loves to let her Poopsie run all over the place, doesn't Mama?" The little dog barked and ran around in circles. Everyone pretended that they were as infatuated with the dog as was Madame.

The butler, a young boy dressed in a ridiculously large set of tails, announced the Chef. "Intesti and his latest bitch," said the boy.

"Oh my darling Chef," said Madame, holding out her hand. She sat on a large throne-like chair in her front parlor. The chair seemed to be made from white marble. She looked quite imposing, as she took up a large volume of cubic square feet. The Chef shuffled up, embarrassed, and kissed her hand.

"Awe crap," he said.

"And who is this *little treat* the Chef has brought us?" snorted Madame Pusillanious.

Standing behind the Chef, blinking in the light, was Tremble. She was, as they say, out of sorts. Her little black dress was crumpled, her hair was confused, and she had red marks all over her neck. In her hand, sloshing back and forth, was a large martini.

The Chef began to say something, but Madame interrupted. "Oh, Chef, save your words, for they are as fleeting as life itself," she said pompously.

A few of the people in her coterie clapped, and one said, "Oh Madame, you should have been a poet."

"I know," said Madame, "I could have been many things. But instead I derive my pleasure from being a patron to young artists. Like young Bingleberry here." At this Madame stuck her nose in the air and shrieked, "Bingleberry!"

The young butler reentered the room. He looked absurd in his tails, which covered his hands and bunched up around his legs.

"Bingleberry is a promising singer," Madame pronounced. "I have taken him under my patronage. Sing something for us, Bingleberry!"

Bingleberry looked skyward and sang for a few minutes. His voice was innocent and sweet and breathtaking. Everyone clapped politely.

"Thank you," said Bingleberry.

"Shut up Bingleberry," said Madame. "No one actually wants to hear you talk."

Just then, Poopsie jumped on a table and knocked over a glass of wine, which splattered on several people, ruining their clothing. Poopsie began lapping up the wine.

"Oh look at Poopsie. Look at my little Poopsie! Poopsie likes the wine, doesn't my little Poopsie," said Madame Pusillanious. She turned to Bingleberry and called out imperiously, "Butler, clean up that wine! And then re-dust my room. I just found several specks of dust that weren't there a few minutes ago. Perhaps if you were a better butler you'd have more time to practice your singing."

Bingleberry wiped up the wine, but had some difficulty doing so because Poopsie kept barking and trying to bite his hand. Madame laughed at this spectacle, and everyone followed suit. Then Bingleberry left the room, crying a little.

After Poopsie finished with the wine, he ran up to the Chef's date, Tremble. He began to bark riotously and jumped up and down with great spastic energy. Tremble tried to shoo him away.

"Poopsie knows something, doesn't Poopsie?" said Madame ecstatically. She turned to the Chef and admonished him, "Chef, really, before you even got here? You boys just can't wait to play with your toys. You are such the Casanova. If I were younger, I'd like to be turned on your spit. Harrumph!"

The great Chef blushed like a child.

Then Madame felt it necessary to brag about her home and decor a bit. "You must meet my new interior designer, Fabulo." Fabulo stood and took a quick bow. He was wearing the smoking jacket and the other things.

"I'm pleased, very pleased," he said in a bad accent constructed from the languages of France, Italy, Spain and other miscellaneous countries. "It is very pleasing for Fabulo to have a client of such power and passion."

"Fabulo is from Italy—the southern part," Madame said proudly. "There is a lot of sun and people tan."

Madame then began a long monologue about the various things she had in her home thanks to Fabulo. Apparently, cemetery artifacts were all the rage, and Madame had displayed great artistic genius by hiring Fabulo to redecorate her house. The chairs were made from headstones that were solid marble and centuries old. The kitchen table was a white piece of marble that had once covered a tomb. There were dozens of marble angels and shrouded urns scattered over every inch of floor space.

Madame took the party to her bedroom. A large aboveground tomb, the type for which the city was famous, had been emptied and fashioned into a bedchamber.

"Isn't it just marvelous," said Madame. "It makes such a quiet sleeping chamber. And I feel deliciously profound sleeping in it." She struck a pose and exhaled, "Ashes to ashes, dust to dust."

Everyone applauded enthusiastically. "You should have been a prophet," said one of her coterie.

"Yes, I know," said Madame. "I could have been many things."

The preservationist, a shrill-looking little balding man with round glasses, happened to peek his head into the bathroom and he screamed in horror. He stumbled back, looking as though he had seen a ghost. "Violated, destroyed, desecrated!" he cried.

The whole group looked around in excitement. Poopsie began to jump up and down and bark and run in circles.

"You have running water," the preservationist bawled. "This house has been desecrated! They ran pipes through these walls, these ancient old walls! I could accept the electricity, but running water! Our ancestors made do for hundreds of years with outhouses, and they left us these precious treasures, these old houses, and you have gutted them for your scatological ease! You monster!"

He would have gone on, and might have dampened the spirit of the group, but Poopsie began to pee on the man's leg. The group cried in laughter and the man went running out of the house, tears streaking down his face.

"Wine makes Poopsie pee," cooed Madame to her dog. "Yes it does. It makes Poopsie pee, doesn't it?"

"That was too much," laughed one of the group. "I might have to put this in my next novel." It was Arthur Holesom, the famous writer. Like most men living in the French district, he was gay.

His wife laughed as well. "I'm afraid you might have picketing tomorrow," said Mrs. Holesom.

"Oh please," said Madame Pusillanious. "You simply have to pay off the right people on the architectural review board."

The crowd went back downstairs. Mr. Holesom, who was constantly seeking young men who needed his attention, was gazing out the window longingly when he spotted the young man whom Chef Intesti had employed as a limousine driver.

"Is that your driver, Intesti?" said Arthur Holesom.

"Yeah," said the Chef. "Worst driver I ever has had. Drinks on the job, rude, and got a smart mouth to boot."

Arthur licked his lips. "He sounds like my type of boy. May I have him?"

Chef Intesti shrugged. "I don't give a crap."

Madame Pusillanious, being a good hostess, was always eager to satisfy her guests. "Bingleberry, call that driver in!" she howled madly.

A few moments later, Ennui was escorted into the house. Like Tremble, he stood there, blinking in the light. His eyes were red and bloodshot, and he held an empty martini glass in his hand.

"We thought we'd take you out of the cold, dear boy," said Madame, holding out her hand to be kissed.

"It's warm outside," said Ennui.

"Well, we thought we'd take you out of the rain," she replied.

"There isn't a cloud in the sky," said Ennui.

"I've been holding my hand out for some time," said

Madame.

"I'm sorry," said Ennui, "but I haven't any spare change."

Madame put her hand down. "Impetuous youth," she grunted. "Haven't you any skill, any talent, so that I can put you under my patronage? Can't you sing, or dance, or paint or write? Can't you play the piano, or the violin?"

"I'm afraid not," said Ennui.

Madame groaned as though she was about to expire. "The youth of today, how rude they are! They refuse to become artists so that I can put them under my patronage."

"I can make an excellent martini," said Ennui.

"Well by all means, bring me one of these martinis," the Madame commanded with an angry flourish.

Ennui was glad to go to the kitchen, for the gaze of Arthur Holesom made him nervous.

Once Ennui had left the room, Madame turned to Tremble and the Chef. "Now my young dear," she said to Tremble. "Other than the fact that you wear a dress that is entirely too short, and your face is too obviously flushed, what do you have to say for yourself?"

The group tittered. Madame often relished the opportunity to practice her rapier-like wit on unsuspecting guests. The Chef seemed entirely uninterested in Tremble, now that his appetite had been sated. He sat down on a marble bench and scratched his crotch.

"I mean, it is altogether too obvious that you are merely an object on which the Chef can satisfy his desires—or should I say, has satisfied his desires," Madame continued. "Why, in my youth I made sure to marry the man in order to at least get his money when he became bored with me. But then again, what a youth I had. I was cultured, and I traveled and all the dignitaries and industrialists in the world were in love with me."

"All I can say," said Tremble, "is that I am very hungry."

The room went still as the coterie anxiously awaited Madame's reply.

"Bravo bravo!" Madame Pusillanious blurted out suddenly. The whole group rose and applauded Tremble. "How profound," the artist murmured. "She has in those words deconstructed existentialism and replaced it with multicultural totalitarianism."

The Chef frowned. "Oh, yeah, I was gonna to cook you somethin at home," he mumbled.

"Really, Intesti," said Madame. "Can it be that the great Chef, the head of an ever-expanding restaurant empire, neglects to feed his dates? Can you be so cheap? Is it possible that you are stingy? I would hate for a cruel assertion like this to get around. And do recall, Intesti, that I own a sizable part of your company. Why can't we get a home-cooked tidbit from our dear friend, Chef Intesti?"

The whole coterie yelled and cheered. Poopsie jumped up and down and yipped and began to pee on the Chef.

Chef Intesti bowed awkwardly. "Alright alright. Crap already. Gimme a few minutes. I'll whip you somethin up. A real killer dish."

Chef Intesti and Tremble went into the kitchen, where they saw Ennui being chased by Arthur Holesom.

"Aren't you married?" Tremble asked Mr. Holesom.

"My wife and I have an *understanding*. It was different back then," said Mr. Holesom.

"Give it a break," said the Chef. Mr. Holesom pouted and left the kitchen. The Chef was sizzling. "Some nerve you gots askin me to cook," he said to Tremble. "Who do you thinks I is?"

"Don't you know how to cook?" asked Tremble. "I mean, there's a restaurant named after you."

"Yeah I does," he belched. "I gots millions in the bank. But they thinkin of me like some damn servant. You's people never gets enough. What the hell is this? A wood burning stove. Awe crap."

The Chef had a look of constipation on his face. He began to rummage through the refrigerator. Ennui, sensing danger, finished making the martinis and left the room with Tremble.

The Chef
gives the party
a culinary creation

In the main room, Ennui approached the throne of Madame Pusillanious and presented her with a martini. The whole room went quiet. Even Poopsie sat reverently. Madame gravely raised the drink to her lips. Then she lowered the drink to the floor. Poopsie approached and took two laps. Everyone gasped in anticipation. Poopsie raised his head and began to yip excitedly.

"Bravo!" cried Madame. "Bravo young man! A martini fit for a queen. I'll pay you a thousand dollars for your martini recipe!"

There was a general hubbub in the room as everyone rushed to taste the martini. Poopsie wasn't very happy at having his martini taken away, and he barked and nipped at the guests.

Then, there was a loud clanging. Bingleberry was ringing a rusted plantation bell that Madame had hung in the dining room. Moments later, Chef Intesti strode in triumphantly, holding a large golden platter covered by a golden lid. He placed the platter on the marble slab table and everyone gathered around. They all "oohed" and "aahed" and said how good it smelled, although they had no idea what it was and could smell nothing.

With a flourish the Chef lifted the lid, revealing a raw chicken with a dozen forks stuck in it. "Chicken à la nude," he proclaimed grandly. "Fridge chilled, air aged, grains of salt and pepper. I'm gonna call it Chicken Pusillanious."

"It's brilliant for its simplicity," gasped Madame Pusillanious. "A stroke of genius! Breaking all conceptions about chicken. He has done for chicken what Adolph Loos did for architecture! Ornament is Evil!"

With that, the group cheered the Chef and struck in, ripping apart the chicken and devouring it greedily. They all moaned in pleasure and worshipped the Chef's ingenuity and genius.

"He has revealed the true essence of the chicken!" cried the artist who painted canvasses white. "The chicken has been hidden for centuries under butter and seasoning and cooking, and he has now freed it. The chicken has been freed!"

They rushed the great Chef and shoved food into his mouth in appreciation of his great service to them, and to humankind.

"Here, have some," Madame Pusillanious spat out rudely, shoving a piece in Tremble's face. "It's supposedly for you." Tremble nodded thankfully, then secretly gave her piece to Poopsie, who ate it and went to a corner and threw up.

During the melee, Ennui sidled up to Fabulo, the interior decorator.

"Say," said Ennui. "That is a very interesting jacket you are wearing."

"Thank you," said Fabulo.

"And those are interesting cuff links."

"Yes they are."

"Then perhaps you could tell me where I could purchase them."

"From any respectable shop in London."

"Perhaps I have something you have been looking for."

"What is that?" asked Fabulo.

"A certain uniform from Angola."

"No, I don't believe so. I am Fabulo. I am not into that sort of fashion."

"The number 3822 doesn't ring a bell?"

"Why should a number ring a bell for Fabulo?"

"Perhaps you like the taste of malt liquor."

"I would never let anything but a martini pass these lips, for they are the lips of Fabulo."

"Perhaps you have something I've been looking for."

"What would that be?"

"A Cadillac that only plays country music."

"Fabulo has a Cadillac, and he loves country music."

"You *love* country music?"

Fabulo wavered a little.

"I would like my things back," said Ennui.

"No way," Fabulo whispered. "I'm on a hot streak with these interior decorator scams. My cell-mate told me how to do these jobs."

"I may turn you in," said Ennui.

"Yeah and you ain't no Bertel Milksop," said Fabulo.

This may have gone on longer, but thankfully a police captain burst into the room.

"Freeze!" yelled the captain.

A crowd of police rushed into the house with guns drawn and immediately began standing around and making themselves drinks.

"Ah-ha!" the captain said to Madame. "Desecrating the cemeteries wasn't enough, was it? Now you must practice voodoo rituals. I wonder what that poor chicken you've sacrificed would think of all this?"

"I demand an explanation!" shrieked Madame Pusillanious.

The captain strode up and lifted Madame's dress, revealing an endless naked rump whiter than milk. It was the size of two large watermelons pushed together. He gave it a firm slap, which made Madame jump, and set her coterie tittering.

"I hereby arrest you for possession of stolen cemetery

property," he said. "And for being annoying, conceited, ignorant and arrogant."

"You can't arrest me for being annoying and those other things," said Madame.

"I can arrest you for anything I want," said the captain. He made a motion and two officers lifted her dress again and delivered a frightening barrage of spankings. Madame squealed with a mixture of horror and delight.

"Those other charges may not stick," said the captain, "but they sound good to me. The stolen cemetery property, however, is going to land you in jail for a long time."

"I didn't buy these," Madame said indignantly. "They came from Fabulo!"

"And just who is this Fabulo?" said the captain. "Describe him to me."

"Why he's an Italian interior decorator. He was here a moment ago. He's the most sought-after decorator in town. *Surely* your house has been decorated by him."

Fabulo of course was nowhere to be seen.

The captain snorted. "The only thing hot in here is this property."

"But I didn't know these objects were stolen," Madame blubbered. "I just thought they were used. That a cemetery was remodeling, or something like that."

"Take her away," the captain ordered. "And arrest all of these other people for being morons. And arrest that dog, too."

"Arrest my little Poopsie?"

"Yes," said the captain. "Arrest the dog for public intoxication, and for being the annoying dog of an annoying woman."

Chef Intesti quickly approached the captain and whispered something in his ear.

"Does that include the banana splits? I love those banana splits you make," said the captain.

"Yeah, all you want," said the Chef.

"Let this man go," said the captain. "And his date, because she has a nice ass, and his driver, because I like his uniform. It looks cute on him. The rest of these, bring 'em downtown."

"But you can't arrest us for being morons," said Arthur Holesom.

"Tell it to the judge," said the captain.

The police dragged Madame Pusillanious and her coterie outside. The officers had difficulty fitting Madame into a squad car. Eventually they stuffed her in the trunk with the lid open and strapped her down with a heavy cord. Once Madame was properly secured, the police lit up their lights and turned on their sirens and disappeared among the crooked streets and fog rolling in off the river.

Chef Intesti
relaxes
after his meal

It had been a long night and Chef Intesti had grown tired. He ordered that Tremble be driven home. However, as they were driving, the Chef began to groan loudly. He clutched his stomach and turned green and moaned, "Crap I feel like I'm gonna die." Then he passed out.

"Is he dead?" Ennui called from the front.

"I hope so," said Tremble. "I don't believe he was going to marry me."

"No, I don't think so," said Ennui. "Should we just drive to the cemetery?"

"Perhaps we should see if he is dead first," said Tremble.

"That's a good idea. Should we stab his side?"

"I wouldn't want to stain the limo," said Tremble. "Or my dress—blood is so difficult for the cleaners to get out."

Ennui pulled into one of the cemeteries for which the city was famous. The tombs were whitish houses for the dead, lining miniature, moonlit alleys.

With some difficulty they pulled Intesti out of the car. One of the tombs had been reopened by grave-robbers, so they pushed his body into it.

"That's the end of that," said Tremble.

"Perhaps we should say something, a eulogy of some sort," said Ennui.

"Allow me. I did win a prize in speech class in seventh grade, you know."

"Please do." Ennui emptied the remnants of his martini in the entrance to the tomb. "May your soul rest in peace," he said gravely.

"That was a very noble gesture," said Tremble. "Sacrificing your martini like that."

Ennui shrugged. "It had grown warm."

The crackle of gunfire echoed through the night air, but it was nothing unusual—a typical outbreak of gang warfare somewhere in the city. The sky glowed red in the distance. It was the normal half-dozen houses burnt nightly by owners who wanted to clear their lots of decrepit historic property.

"Here lies Chef Intesti," Tremble began. "He was one of the noblest men with whom I have ever been with. He owned seven restaurants, a publicly traded company, and a fine limousine. Everywhere he went, people adored and admired him. Like all men though, he had a fault, for fault made him man—he was rather gassy. Other than that, he would have made a perfect husband. He had all the characteristics of a great and noble husband. He would cheat freely on me. In return, he would give me unlimited manicures, pedicures, facials and shopping sprees. He was a true soul mate. But now he is dead, done in by his own cooking. He was not of this world, lord. He was like an ignorant child. He had forgotten that chicken should be fully cooked or you can die from eating it."

Ennui was a little choked up. "That was the most moving speech I have ever heard. How can I ever hope to marry you, when your heart was once touched by a man such as this?"

This type of nonsense might have continued between our dear couple, but they were silenced by a loud groaning coming from the tomb.

Ennui put his hand over Tremble's mouth to silence her. "Are you sure he was dead?" he said softly.

"Was that important?" Tremble whispered.

Ennui went to the limousine and retrieved a flashlight. "My dear girl, let me give you this gift, this gift of marriage," he whispered in her ear. "On my word, you shall have Chef Intesti engaged to you this very night."

Ennui disappeared into the tomb. He turned on the flashlight and shined it into Intesti's face. Intesti groaned and turned on the marble slab. "Where is I?" he moaned.

"You are dead, in the tomb," said Ennui in the deepest voice he could muster.

"Crap," groaned the Chef. "Who is you?"

"I am the Angel Gabriel," said Ennui.

"Which one was that?"

"That is one of your many sins, not paying attention in catechism."

"Oh, I gots many sins," cried the Chef. "Is that the light I see? I afraid to go to the light."

"You should be afraid, for you would be sentenced to hell."

"What's in hell?"

"Your sentence would be determined by your sins. Thus, you will be forced to gourmet cook, for all eternity!"

Here the Chef cried and groaned so loudly that a passing citizen would think that the dead were rising from their tombs.

"Yes, cooking is the job of the servant," Ennui boomed. "But on earth, foolish men have made servants kings, and kings servants. No such nonsense is allowed in god's realm I can assure you."

The Chef groaned and cried and slobbered. "Please, Angel Gabriel, you gotta cut me a break."

"You deserve no such chance! But since the Angel Gabriel is in a good mood today, he will give you one—only if you rectify the last wrong you have committed. You have debased the creatures that god made to stand for beauty and virtue. You have turned them into receptacles for your dirty pleasures."

"Yeah yeah, the girl, Flimple."

"You must promise to take this girl as your wife."

"Awe please, not her!"

"And if you don't, I will see that you die a frightful and grisly death-by-shredding in your restaurant! But if you keep your promise, when your hour comes, perhaps we will spare you from an eternity in the *kitchen!*"

At the mention of that last word, the Chef groaned and writhed in pain. Then the flashlight's battery began to fade. "Light's fadin," breathed out the Chef. "That mortal world is takin a hold of me. Thanks, Angel Gabriel. Thanks a bunch." And with that, the Chef passed out again.

Ennui emerged from the grave, hurried Tremble into the limousine, and slowly drove off.

"Well, I believe that about does it," said Ennui. "Here are the keys to your new house."

"That was nice of you," said Tremble. "Perhaps that was the nicest thing you have ever done for me. If I become married to Intesti as a result of this, perhaps I will marry you."

"That would be quite nice," said Ennui.

Tremble
receives
her first guest

They drove back to Intesti's house, which was one of the old mansions on St. Withburga Avenue. Ennui went to the kitchen and found some gin and vermouth which he used to make martinis. Then they sat in Intesti's living room. It was a very grand room, with an airy crystal chandelier, lofty ceilings, beautiful plaster moldings, and a shag rug.

"This is very civilized," said Tremble. "I could get used to these surroundings, with a few adjustments here and there."

"The Chef should be coming along any minute now," said Ennui. "Are you ready to be engaged?"

"I am a little nervous," said Tremble. "After all, this is the moment all girls dream of ever since they begin seeing advertisements."

Presently the Chef came stumbling through the door. He was a sight. Dust and dirt had whitened his hair, and scraps of indescribable things clung to his clothing. He collapsed at Tremble's feet. "I back from the dead," he gasped. "I escape from the tomb. The ghosts was talkin to me."

"Oh, please," said Tremble. "I've heard that one so many times before. You've kept me waiting here for quite some time, and very rudely, too."

"Hey," said the Chef, grabbing her hand. "You gotta marry me. I'll change my ways. I'll devote me to makin you a happy broad."

"As for the marriage part," said Tremble, "that does sound agreeable as it involves community property. But as to the part of devoting your life to making me happy, that would become rather tiresome, having somebody bother over me constantly."

But the Chef didn't hear her words. He was too busy slobbering and crying on her hand.

"We must go to an all-night wedding chapel at once," said Tremble, "before I change my mind."

"Yeah yeah," cried the Chef. "Right now. You gotta save me from the kitchen."

And with that Ennui nodded to himself quietly and sipped his martini. He was sitting comfortably in a gilded chair. The couple would get married that night. The story appeared to be over. Tremble would finally achieve her dream of marrying a wealthy, indifferent man. As for Ennui, what were his dreams? He really didn't have any. He did want to get his clothing back, but as long as he had a fresh supply of martinis, any sort of life would be palatable.

While Ennui was lost in his reveries, there was a loud crash and a hairy ape-man was seen coming through a large French door. He wore a loin-cloth of dishrags and held a large dish-scraper in his hand. He immediately plunged the scraper into the Chef's heart.

The great Chef uttered his last words, "awe crap." He let out a long, slow fart and died.

"Bertel, look what you've done," yelled Tremble. "You've killed my husband-to-be."

Apparently, Bertel's full rage was vented in this one quick and violent act, and he slowly came to his senses. "Cadillac—ungha ungha ungha—wine—ungha ungha—dishes—ungha," he mouthed, slowly and with much difficulty.

"Yes, yes, whatever," said Tremble. She stomped her foot on the floor and pouted. "You've murdered my fiancé. Now what am I to do? I invite you out, and look how you behave. No wonder you have such difficulty finding people to enjoy your car with you. You are so antisocial."

Bertel looked at the dead body. Then he put his head down and shuffled out the front door. It is a tragic sight to see a man steeped in utter defeat, no matter his crime.

Ennui continued to sip his martini calmly from the comfort of his chair. "Now what are we going to do?"

"Well, I don't want to hang around here," said Tremble. "Not with this dead body and all. It's bleeding all over the place. And his tongue is sticking out horribly, and his eyes staring at me. It's indecent."

"Yes, I agree," said Ennui. "It is rather rude of the Chef. One would think he'd be a better host, being in the hospitality business and so forth. But we do have the limo. Perhaps we could drive over to Captain Antonneil's for a bite to eat. I didn't dare touch that raw chicken Intesti served, and I find myself quite hungry. By all means they'd run us a tab if they saw us arrive in the limo."

"I'm not that hungry," said Tremble. "But I could be persuaded to have a light appetizer, perhaps, and of course some wine. And Captain Antonneil's is the second most expensive restaurant in town, so it is bound to be almost as good as Intesti's."

"Of course."

"And they do make excellent martinis."

Ennui looked sad.

"Not as good as yours, of course," Tremble quickly put in.

"Yes of course," said Ennui, brightening.

HUMAN DETRITUS

The papers
break the news

Over the next several days, anyone who awoke in Tremble and Ennui's fair city and retrieved their paper, assuming, that is, that their paper had not been stolen, would have found no articles out of the ordinary.

It was the same litany of ancient mansions collapsing on vagrant residents, warfare erupting between rival gangs, widespread drunkenness among the citizenry causing them to do idiotic things, landlord-paid arsonists torching neighborhoods, cemeteries being robbed en masse and their artifacts shipped elsewhere to decorate houses of the socially conscious, politicians stuffing their pockets with bribes and gourmands stuffing their faces with food, all set amidst a ceaseless season of society parties where the blue bloods proudly traced their ancestries to human garbage dumped out of France centuries ago.

But for the reader interested in the activities of Tremble and Ennui, perhaps a few articles are worth mention, in a paraphrased form.

CHEF INTESTI MURDERED!

Chef Intesti, world famous for his cooking empire, was found dead in his St. Withburga Avenue mansion this morning... neighbors reported seeing a large ape leaving the residence... police confirmed that prints on the instrument of death, a dish scraper, are indeed ape prints... animals at zoo are being fingerprinted... zoo officials declined to comment... prosecutors said they will seek life imprisonment for the guilty ape... angry gourmet food community claimed cover-up at zoo and wants death penalty... food community said ape meat would be best prepared by sautéing in lemon and butter, washed down with a "robust, almost primitive" Bordeaux...

Sharing the front page was a picture of flames, under which the following article appeared:

ANGRY ORPHANS
BURN INTESTI'S!

Intesti's restaurant, known worldwide for serving the nouveau of nouveau cuisine, has been burned to a simmering pile by a mob of angry orphans... grilling of restaurant apparently retribution for being stood up by Intesti...

The fine journalists of the city, dedicated to ferreting out the truth at all costs, had done a commendable job. Therefore, one is compelled to paraphrase a few other articles that may be of interest to the reader.

SOCIALITE ARRESTED IN CEMETERY THEFT RING!

Madame Pusillanious, a prominent French district socialite was arrested late Thursday night for allegedly stealing priceless cemetery artifacts... Madame's dog, "Poopsie," was pepper-sprayed and handcuffed after urinating on the arresting officer... Pusillanious under psychiatric evaluation after claims of royalty and the existence of a Italian decorator named Fabulo... several prominent French district residents arrested in melee at House of Pusillanious following arrest of Madame... notable artists, authors and musicians among those arrested... artist community protesting arrests by ceasing all production of art... city populace cheers cessation of art and arrest of annoying people... mayor, boosted by opinion polls concerning arrests, declared "we'll keep arresting annoying artists, writers and intellectuals until the streets are once again safe"... several of those arrested treated for food poisoning by prison doctors...

And then there was an article about the Chef in the prominent New York paper. It was lengthy, and unfortunately literary, so its summary will be kept short:

EDMUND INTESTI, CHEF

Edmund Intesti, Chef, dead at 40... culinary world mourns loss of leading "shooting star"... legions of dedicated fans flocked to smoking hulk of restaurant to pay their respects... mourners took burning embers and sizzled animal parts as mementos... Intesti embraced minimalism in his last meal, a "breathtaking" shift, according to food critics... Intesti called a "daring culinary pioneer" after preparation of last dish, which sickened several people and killed two... leading food critic declared, "Intesti risked even death pushing the boundaries of food, how many of us are so brave? He was a great man."

And that was about it, except for one short little article hiding in a corner:

MISSING: SON OF
LOCAL BUSINESSMAN

Bertel Milksop, missing since Tuesday... described by father as a "short, hairy, squatty thing in an overpriced car"... reward offered by father for information leading to location of son... reward increased to $50 by father... father said, "It looks like he's gone. Oh well. I had a dog that ran away once, and it never came back either."

And while the mighty presses rolled and the papers flowed—waves of information spreading over the far, wide land—where were Tremble and Ennui? One can see Bertel Milksop squatting amongst the trees in his loin-cloth, ancient and godlike, obscured like a ruin in the wilderness. One can see a man driving around the city in a black Cadillac, listening to country music, which he has grown to like. One can see Chef Intesti, his body in an ice cooler in the mortuary, his soul gone to the place where souls go.

But Tremble and Ennui moved too fast and hid too completely to be so easily found. However, like all things, they eventually returned home. When they got home they slept—in innocent, childlike seclusion. For in their neighborhood the real world was but an abstraction. Fashion and culture came and went, and came and went again, without anyone knowing. Countries declared war and made peace, and declared war again, and no one heard the news. National chain stores—the ambassadors spreading the latest of western culture—peeked down those narrow alleys, shook their heads, and settled elsewhere.

And likewise, no thought penetrated the mind of Tremble. She had forgotten to vomit out the enormous meal she ate at Captain Antonneil's, and so her body seized on the food and put her into hibernation. And for Ennui, he had consumed such a monstrous number of martinis that it took several days for the vapors to escape his body.

When Ennui finally awoke, he saw that Tremble was not to be disturbed, so he went about his business freely, which was not wise.

Ennui takes
a wife

Words appeared out of the darkness. Tremble began to awake.

"Tremble," Ennui whispered like a ghost.

"Leave me alone," Tremble mumbled, eyes still closed.

"Tremble," Ennui repeated. "Do you have large breasts?"

"Yes."

"You do?"

"I do."

"What was that?"

"I do," said Tremble, more loudly.

Tremble felt a pen being put into her hand, and heard the pen being scratched against paper.

She woke with a shot. "Ennui!"

There was another man in the room with Ennui. The man was dressed in a black suit and appeared to be observing the signature. Tremble yanked her hand away and grabbed the marriage contract, which she tore into shreds. "Ennui, I will not marry you."

"But you already said *I do*," said Ennui. "And on top of that, you are unclothed, which must be rather embarrassing in the company of a stranger."

Tremble snatched the closest thing at hand and tied it around her. It was a drape that Ennui had stolen from Captain Antonneil's, because he felt it didn't go with the decor.

"I most certainly did not say I do," said Tremble. "I mean I did say it, but not in the way you mean. Now who is this man?"

"Justice of the peace, ma'am," said the man.

"Well run along," said Tremble. "There is no marriage occurring today I can assure you. Shoo away little fly. Don't listen to what this boy has told you."

"But you promised you'd marry me if I got you engaged to the Chef," said Ennui. "And a promise is a promise."

"I said I'd marry you if I became married to the Chef," said Tremble.

"Hmmf," said Ennui. "Perhaps you are correct. But you did at least become engaged to the Chef. So therefore I am at least owed an engagement."

Tremble groaned and dove under the sheets. "Oh Ennui," she cried. "I will never marry you. Never never never never! I can't believe you tried to trick me again."

"You wouldn't marry me even if I had a million dollars?"

"No, never!"

"What if I had a million dollars and my smoking jacket and cuff links?"

"Most certainly not!"

"What if I made you a martini?"

Tremble softened a bit. "Perhaps I'd think about it."

So Ennui made some martinis. They gave one to the justice of the peace, who proclaimed it excellent, which meant a lot coming from a justice of the peace. He was a little man with a quiet air about him. After a few martinis the justice became reflective. "I often try to think why people get married," he mused.

"I'm sure it has something to do with primates, or other animals," Tremble said. "Marriage is just so primitive and useless. Imagine, having to wake up to the same person every morning. How horrid." Tremble shivered.

"Yet, waking to a different person each morning, or to no person at all is even more horrid, to use your term, to some people," said the justice.

"Oh, please," Tremble groaned. "Marriage has much in common with apes picking bugs off each other's hides—grooming—that sort of thing. And copulation. And raising horrible little children who bother you until you die."

"I think it may have something to do with love," Ennui put in.

Tremble laughed rudely.

"You may be right," said the justice. "Love is a jealous thing that demands possession. Haven't you ever loved anything?"

"Well, let's see," Tremble thought out loud. "There was a pair of shoes that I absolutely loved. And I was very possessive of them. I wouldn't let any of my friends see them because I was afraid they would buy the same pair. But then the shoes went out of style, and I threw them out. I don't think I ever actually wore them."

Thankfully the conversation was interrupted by a tremendous pounding on the door. It sounded as though great sides of beef were being tossed up against the rickety shack.

Mr. Flatulus
shows charity
to his tenants

The voice of Mr. Flatulus was heard. "Open up. Open up that door."

"Or what, you'll huff and puff and blow the house down?" Ennui yelled.

"Don't provoke him," said Tremble to Ennui. "You'll just make him sweat more."

"I'm tired of this rent thing being held constantly over my head," said Ennui. "Such poor taste, continually demanding that we pay him. You'd think he'd have something better to do."

"Don't get into a tizzy," said Tremble. "We'll just pawn something off of the limousine. There's sure to be something worth a few dollars. The tires, or the hubcaps, or the engine or something."

Ennui went to the window and peered out. He didn't say anything. He just stared silently.

"What, is the limo gone?" said Tremble.

"No, not quite," said Ennui.

"Has it been stripped?"

"Well, sort of," said Ennui.

The pounding at the door grew more thunderous. "Open up!" yelled Mr. Flatulus. "I know you're in there. I can smell the booze!"

"What's the magic word?" Ennui yelled back.

Mr. Flatulus let loose an unprintable string of profanities.

"No, that's not it," Ennui replied.

"Is there anything left of the limo?" asked Tremble impatiently. "We could at least sell it for scrap!"

"I'm afraid that isn't possible," said Ennui.

Tremble groaned. She went to the window and pushed Ennui aside. "Oh drat," she said.

"Yes, it couldn't be worse," said Ennui. "Squatters!"

They saw that a large family had moved into the limousine after the wheels and radio had been stolen. The family seemed quite comfortably settled. Laundry was hanging from the boomerang-shaped antenna. The men were grilling several chickens in the space that used to house the engine. The trunk had been filled with water, and four children were being scrubbed ear to toe by the mother. They splashed about and rubbed their soap-covered heads. Inside, a group of teenage girls was watching cable news.

"Well, get them out," Tremble shrieked. "It's not their limo."

"Afraid it can't be done," said the justice, who had joined them at the window. "Once they move in and establish residency, they have legal possession of the property." A postman walked by and delivered the morning mail to the car's glove box.

"Then you deal with Flatulus," said Tremble to Ennui. "I am certainly not to blame for our predicament. I didn't lose Bertel's wallet, or his Cadillac, or the limo."

"Gladly," Ennui sniffed.

Mr. Flatulus was about to embark on another round of door pounding, when the door suddenly swung open.

"I'm afraid you're trespassing on our property," said Ennui. "You'll have to leave at once!"

Mr. Flatulus' fat lips blew and sputtered spastically before he was able to reply. "Your property? This is my property!"

"Oh, it is?" said Ennui calmly. "Then why are you outside and we are inside if it is your property?"

"Because I am renting it to you," cried Mr. Flatulus.

"How absurd," Ennui sniffed. He turned around to Tremble. "Did you hear that, he says he is renting to us!"

Tremble cackled.

"Haven't you heard that the country has gone communist?" said Ennui. "Therefore the government owns this property, and I demand that you step off of it, you ugly capitalist. Otherwise, I'm afraid they'll make good use of you at the glue factory."

The words seemed to stun Mr. Flatulus like a blast to the head, but he shook it loose and demanded, "You pay rent right now or else."

"Oh, it's rent you want," said Ennui. "I wish you had said so. Let's think about this. What is rent? It is payment exchanged for temporary use of a property. And what is payment, other than money? And what is money, other than the symbol of work and existence..."

Mr. Flatulus had somehow produced a shotgun. "You won't pay, so I will give you the worst!"

"Oh, please," said Tremble, coming forward. "The worst? Eviction?"

"No, something far worse," Mr. Flatulus rumbled. Beads of sweat made their way down his swollen face like insects crawling out from beneath a rock.

"Death?" said Ennui.

"Far worse than that, my little children," said Mr. Flatulus ominously. "I'm going to report you to social services!"

A little scream burst out of Tremble before she was able to put her hand to her mouth. This was indeed a cruel and heartless threat, only to be unleashed by the most heartless of men.

Mr. Flatulus lowered his shotgun. "That's right. If your little boy hadn't smarted off, maybe I would have given you another day, but now—" and here Mr. Flatulus pulled his finger across his throat and then pretended to dial a number with it, "social services gets a call to visit 231 Soraparu. I'm going to have social workers crawling all over this place."

Mr. Flatulus floated backwards and the door drifted shut. A death-like, chilling silence crept through the house.

"I can see I'm of no help here," said the justice of the peace. He shot back the rest of the martini and hopped out a window.

"He wouldn't," said Tremble to Ennui.

"I'm afraid he would," said Ennui to Tremble.

"How could he? Just because we haven't paid rent?"

"We are talking about a man who uses tear gas as an

eviction notice."

The horror of the moment began to settle into their bones. Tremble crawled into bed and began to shiver. "It's so cold in here."

"I fear they would try to reform you," said Ennui.

Tremble shook in fear.

"They would try to make a responsible citizen of you," Ennui added.

Tremble grew pale.

"They would try to teach you family values."

Tremble's eyes opened wide.

"They would make you get a job," he declared.

Tremble shrieked and pulled the sheets over her head.

Ennui picked himself up and made a fresh martini. "Oh, but I'm not afraid," he said. "I mean, I was shocked at first, but we merely just need to find a plan. Right now, it seems as though we should flee the country. Now where can we charter a private jet?"

"With what money?" cried Tremble from beneath the sheets.

"Yes, that's right. Lack of money. That's why we're in this predicament. Plus, foreigners are so vomitous. They always want to speak their own language. Perhaps we could move to a cheaper place?"

"Cheaper than free? How?"

"What about your welfare check?"

"I cashed it already. It'll be three weeks until the next one."

They sat in silence for some time. Finally, Tremble's head appeared from beneath the sheets. "There's only one thing to do," she said. "I'll have to move home."

Ennui laughed a loud, maniacal laugh. "Why, that is a fate worse than death."

"My parents have a very nice little house," said Tremble, standing up proudly. "Perhaps I will go live there. And perhaps I'll come back one day to visit this city, and we'll see you. I'll tell my children not to give money to bums who drink gin and beg for change, because they'll only spend it on liquor."

"That's the only reason I *do* give money to bums," said Ennui, "Because I know they'll spend it properly."

"Oh, Ennui, just get out."

"You can't be in the presence of one who will stand up to adversity? I am quite disappointed at your lack of resolution. I'm afraid it hints at inferior breeding."

"Get out, Ennui. I can't stand the sight of you!"

"That is rather harsh," said Ennui. "I know I look ridiculous in this chauffeur outfit, but I did it for your sake."

"Get out get out get out!"

"You are becoming quite shrill," said Ennui. "I fear this is becoming a domestic dispute. Perhaps we have been among our neighbors for too long. And I have too much class to become involved in such a pedestrian affair..."

An empty bottle of gin was hurled at Ennui's head.

"That was quite close," said Ennui, inching towards the door.

Another followed, and then another, and Ennui slipped through the door, avoiding death. And as he had done so many times before, he sauntered down the street, alone.

"I might actually take offense one of these days at her lack of hospitality," said Ennui to himself.

Tremble gets religion

Tremble was a trapped animal. She wandered around the apartment, agitated. She flipped through various fashion magazines, but threw them all aside. She tried on different outfits. Nothing felt right. She tore them all off in disgust and wanted to feel fat. So she put on her muumuu.

And then she got into bed, and sleep crept over her.

How long she slept, she didn't know...

Eventually, she found herself listening to a loud, efficient rapping at the door. Her head was still foggy, and she wondered if she was dreaming.

"Open up, open up. There's no need to be afraid," called out a voice.

Tremble slowly opened the door. Standing there was a young lady dressed in a very proper blue suit. The lady wore thick, foggy glasses and she was looking down at a clipboard. "This is 231 Soraparu, is it not?" said the lady.

"Perhaps," said Tremble

"It is hard to tell," said the lady. "Some of the letters on the door have been badly damaged by gunfire. Is it 231 Soraparu?"

"It depends. Who are you?" said Tremble.

"I'm Miss Gruntles, from social services. And do please speak up, ma'am," said the lady. "It's very hard to hear over your seven children. See if you can quiet them. Try tossing them some food."

"I don't have seven children," said Tremble.

"Well, if this is 231 Soraparu, you certainly do. I have the records right here. It is from the computer, and the computer never lies. And there is no reason to be embarrassed by having seven children produced by at least a dozen fathers. You are clearly a product of your environment, and that is nothing to be ashamed of. Growing up in ignorance and poverty, and not knowing that when a boy puts his thingy in you that a baby will come is no shame. I understand—you see, I just received my quadruple doctorate in social work."

Tremble was unable to reply.

"Now, come along. There's no time for dilly-dallying. I have two hundred more cases to attend to today. And I need to take you to your case worker. She is a very prominent lady who has graciously volunteered her time. And she hates to wait."

"But I need to change," said Tremble.

"Nonsense," said Miss Gruntles. "I see you are wearing your muumuu—good. Obesity is also a dreadful problem in the inner city. With all the fatty food you eat, it is no wonder that you welfare mothers grow to such a size. But I don't look down on you, as I took several courses in weight diversity acceptance."

"I'm not about to go anywhere," said Tremble with some indignity, stomping her foot.

"But you must," said Miss Gruntles. "It is now required of anyone receiving benefits. Somehow you slipped through the cracks, and if not for the valiant efforts of a Mr. Flatulus on your behalf, you might never have received the help you needed. That man is a godsend."

"A curse on you, Flatulus!" Tremble muttered to herself.

"And don't tell me any fibs about having to watch over your children, Miss—" and here the social worker consulted her notes. "Miss White. There's no need for illusions between us. We all know that the children are raised by their grandmother while you get high. And I'm not going to let you get your crack pipe before we go. I am not about to be an enabler, you see. Now come along or I will have to have more social workers assist me," said Miss Gruntles firmly.

Tremble was led to an old station wagon and told to climb into the back. Miss Gruntles jumped in and began driving at a high rate of speed through the narrow, crooked streets.

"How is it back there?" yelled Miss Gruntles. "I need to ask, because I took several classes in compassion training. I am sorry that you have to ride in the back, but due to your obese state, it would be impossible to fit you up front."

"What?" cried Tremble. "I don't have that big of an ass," she thought to herself. She felt like crying. The back of the wagon was littered with flower pots and dog hair. Parts of the wagon were rusted through, and Tremble could see the road underneath.

"This is Mrs. Hemoglobin's car," Miss Gruntles went on. "She is so generous to let me borrow it. I'm afraid you wouldn't have fit in my car. It's on the small side."

They arrived at a large mansion on St. Withburga Avenue. Miss Gruntles pushed a button on the car's visor, and a rusty iron gate screeched open. They drove in and stopped under an ornate port-cochere. Miss Gruntles hopped out of the car and made her way to the rear door of the station wagon. She put all her might into pulling the handle, and finally the door creaked open with the groaning of old age. Tremble tumbled to the ground.

"Here we are," said Miss Gruntles breathlessly. "The house of Mrs. Hemoglobin. I have to go now. Mrs. Hemoglobin will have one of her maids drive you back I'm sure."

And at this point Miss Gruntles made her way with unusual haste to her car. It was a brown Corolla that had been completely overtaken by rust. She jumped in and the tin can hopped to life with a great deal of sputtering and smoke. She and the car slowly drifted down the driveway and out the gate. "Mrs. Hemoglobin will take good care of you," cried Miss Gruntles as she pulled onto St. With-burga Avenue, narrowly avoiding a streetcar.

Tremble approached a large door fitted with intricate leaded glass. Her muumuu swayed in a breeze. She was at a loss on what to do. By this time, Ennui would have secured two martinis. But she did like the mansion. It was a huge pile of rustic stone blocks, Moroccan pillars, balus-tered balconies and stained glass and arches. A nice yard sloped down from the house to the iron fence. In front of the house were the gnarled oaks which made a tunnel over the avenue. Her spirits picked up slightly. Perhaps there was money inside.

She noticed, however, that the place did need a bit of touching up. The flowerbeds and gardens were overgrown and the grass needed clipping. Also, several of the upstairs windows were broken and the copper gutters were coming off the building.

She pulled a chain and heard a deep bell resound through the house, followed by the crashing of glass and a long groan.

After several minutes, the door creaked open, but no one appeared to be there. Then she looked down and saw a small boy, perhaps nine or ten years of age, dressed in a black servant's uniform.

"Yes ma'am," he said. "How can I help you?"

"I don't know," said Tremble. "I don't quite know why I'm here."

"If you want my opinion, ma'am," said the boy, "give him up. He's very poor, and you need somebody with money, from the look of your clothes. He can't take care of himself, much less a woman."

"Give whom up?" said Tremble.

"Mr. Hemoglobin," said the boy with utmost sincerity.

"I don't know a Mr. Hemoglobin, or a Mrs. Hemoglobin," said Tremble. "I was just picked up from my house and dropped off here by someone by the name of Miss Gruntles."

The boy screwed up his face, confused. "You're not a welfare mother. You're a snotty girl." Then the boy giggled to himself.

"What are you laughing at?" Tremble said crossly.

"Nothing," said the boy.

"Is that my Miss White?" called out a shrill, brittle woman's voice. "Is that my Miss White? Show her in. Show her into the front parlor at once I tell you."

The boy rolled his eyes and motioned for Tremble to follow. He closed the door and Tremble found herself in a dusty foyer. It had marble black and white checkered flooring, a small crystal chandelier, and a high plaster ceiling that was flaking. The walls were papered with scenes of soldiers in gray defeating soldiers in blue.

The boy, Holmes, was standing on a white square, and Tremble was standing on a black square. "Please follow me," he said. Tremble made a step forward, but Holmes stamped his little foot and said, "Halt!"

Tremble looked at him confused, and Holmes said, "You're not walking on the right squares. Pawns can only move forward, and queens can only move straight or diagonal. Those are the rules. You are the queen—the welfare queen of course—and I am the pawn."

Tremble then stepped forward several steps. And Holmes moved accordingly, until they moved off the check-erboard floor and into the front parlor.

Just before they entered, Holmes motioned for Tremble to bend down. "Once, Mrs. Hemoglobin cut herself, and the blood came out blue," he whispered.

"Did not," said Tremble.

"Did too," said Holmes. "Saw it myself. It came out blue and ruined my shirt."

"You're telling a lie," said Tremble. "Why would you say such a thing?"

"Because how else could I get you to lean down so I can look down your muumuu," said the boy.

"Hmmf," said Tremble as she straightened up. "You obviously knew I had large breasts. I can't help you wanting to view them." That made Tremble feel better.

They entered the parlor. It was a cavernous pastel green room. The floor was covered with a threadbare carpet and the windows with frayed gold curtains. Gaudy Victorian furniture with gross bulges and carvings was scattered throughout the place. The fireplace was a black Italian marble monstrosity topped by two candelabras and a tarnished brass clock. On the walls were dull paintings of dull-looking men and woman, all of whom were distinguished by having very large ears. Tremble's eyes looked at the portraits and the furnishings and finally made it to a little old lady sitting very properly in a high-

backed chair. She had very large ears as well. She wore a
pink hat, a dress of pink lace, and little pink shoes. And
she had a proper china tea set laid out. Her features were
all very sharp and small, and they poked out from a pattern of well-arranged wrinkles.

"Holmes, show her in," said the lady again.

"Follow me," said Holmes. He walked into the room,
following an elaborate pattern in the rug. Tremble walked
straight but Holmes hissed at her to follow him on the
pattern. They walked in this manner for a few minutes,
turning this way and that, until they reached the end.

"Enough of your games, Holmes," said Mrs. Hemoglobin. "Just sit the poor mother down. Imagine, having
seven children pass through those hips. It's amazing
you're able to walk, poor girl."

Tremble sat down in the chair indicated.

"I know, I know, you're admiring my beautiful house,"
said Mrs. Hemoglobin, waving her hand quickly in the
air. "It isn't as big as it looks, though. Romanesque struc-
tures never are. We have only twenty-three rooms here,
but somehow we fit."

"It's very nice," said Tremble politely.

"Yes, yes, but the street isn't what it used to be," Mrs.
Hemoglobin prattled on. "All the old families have left.
And the nouveau riche, of course, moved in. Despicable
people, with all sorts of despicable things going on. Why,

just down the street we had a murder, if you can believe it. Actually, I'm sure murder is something you are used to in your neighborhood, but it caused quite a stir here. A famous chef, no less—Chef Intesti. Murdered by an ape, although I witnessed a little strumpet and the limo driver leave. I think they had something to do with it, but of course the police are only too ready to tie the case up and pin it on the ape."

"That's very shocking," said Tremble.

"Was it? I'm sure the police have better things to do than to track down who killed this or that chef." Then Ms. Hemoglobin looked around and leaned close. "But secretly many of us were glad that Intesti came to that end. There were all sorts of vile rumors about him. I heard he kept a small male chicken in his possession, for instance. And his money wasn't seasoned, you know. He had only become wealthy in the last decade. You know what I mean."

"I'm afraid I don't," said Tremble.

"Have some tea," said Mrs. Hemoglobin, abruptly changing course. Then she added, with her hand fluttering over her breast, "Oh, forgive me dear girl. You probably don't know what tea is, do you? Well, tea is a drink made from the leaves of a plant named Thea sinensis, grown in the Far East. It tastes wonderful, especially with some sugar and honey. You might be thinking of marijuana, but I'm afraid that's a slang use of the word tea. I can say that for sure because my family has been drinking tea for over three hundred years. Why, they've been drinking it in this parlor for a century. Some say that is why we live so long."

She handed Tremble a cup, which Tremble took, but it was so brittle that it shattered as she tried to raise it to her mouth. The tea went all over her muumuu.

"Oh my," said Mrs. Hemoglobin. "Those cups have been in the family for over two hundred years. They tend to do that from time to time. Be careful not to cut yourself, dear. Please do pick up the pieces, will you? And I do hope the tea doesn't stain the carpet. It's an original Pazyryk."

Tremble got on her knees and gathered the pieces. She was soaked from the tea and feeling miserable. The rug was so threadbare that the hardwood floor showed through. She began to sneeze ferociously from the dust.

Presently there was a loud crashing sound coming from upstairs. A man shouted drunkenly, "Hey, what you doing down there Alga?" It was Mr. Hemoglobin calling down.

"I'm busy with my social work," Mrs. Hemoglobin called up in a shrill voice.

There was a uneven howl from upstairs and then all went quiet.

"Now," Mrs. Hemoglobin declared, slapping her bony white hands on her bony knees. "Let's talk about getting you off of welfare."

"But I really don't want to get off of welfare," said Tremble.

"Of course you do," said Mrs. Hemoglobin. "You see, what you suffer from is a lack of self-esteem. And everyone knows that a job will give you self-esteem. A job will empower you," she declared patriotically, with a shake of her little white fist. Her lips pursed with determination at those last words.

"Have you ever held a job?" Tremble asked.

"Why of course not," said Mrs. Hemoglobin, repulsed at the question. "It is not proper for a lady to work."

"My thoughts exactly," said Tremble.

"But you can't continue to live off the government," said Mrs. Hemoglobin with some scorn. "It's very un-American."

"Then perhaps I can marry a wealthy husband," said Tremble.

"Please, my dear," said Mrs. Hemoglobin. She put her hand to her head. "I try to reach out to you people, and look how I am ridiculed. Oh, a martyr I am, positively a martyr. I pray to the saints every day." She looked to the sky and cried out, "St. Withburga, give me strength and guidance!"

Tremble looked confused.

"St. Withburga, my dear—the virgin," explained Mrs. Hemoglobin. "We should all follow her example."

"We should all be virgins?" Tremble asked. "The human race would die out pretty quickly."

"No my dear, she wasn't canonized just because she was a virgin. Please don't make me fear that centuries of civilized, christian education has gone to waste. Don't tell me that we have named our streets in vain. Don't tell me that we have vanquished the heathens for nothing."

Tremble gave her a blank stare.

"St. Withburga was sainted because when they dug her up over three hundred years after her death, her body had not decomposed, of course," said Mrs. Hemoglobin with some impatience. "They say that her limbs were still flexible and her body fresh. However, the bodies of Sisters Sexburga and Ermenilda, buried with her, were reduced to dust, poor things."

"Sister Sexburga?" said Tremble.

"Never mind the names," said Mrs. Hemoglobin hotly. "The important thing is that she is a saint, and therefore we should pray to her."

"I really don't understand," said Tremble. "It all sounds macabre to me."

"Oh my dear, you really don't have the capacity to understand anything do you? That's why you are here.

The world is changing so fast, and you are about to be cut off."

"Cut off?"

"Yes, my dear. You see, welfare has been reformed. But don't fret, it's all in the name of family values."

There was a loud crashing sound that grew closer and closer. Mr. Hemoglobin was falling down the stairs again. He landed in the marble checkered foyer. Holmes appeared with a board, and using it as a leverage device, he was able to pry Mr. Hemoglobin to his feet.

"Thanks, Holmes," Mr. Hemoglobin slurred.

The nobility
of the upper class
is put on display

Mr. Hemoglobin was a portly old wreck. His face and nose were swollen with liquor, and his mustache and hair were big, bushy and a filthy shade of white. He wore a Confederate uniform that would not have fit, except that moths had eaten several large holes in it. Holmes led him out of the foyer, but it took longer because a king can only move one square at a time, and Mr. Hemoglobin was having trouble with his balance.

After Mr. Hemoglobin reached the end of the path on the carpet, he stared unsteadily at Tremble. His eyes narrowed and then got wide and then narrowed again. His lips and tongue curled lecherously.

After much effort, he let out a noise. "Heh!"

"Can't you see that I am busy," Mrs. Hemoglobin screeched. "This poor girl has seven children, and undoubtedly is dying for some drugs, and I am doing my best to get her off of welfare. Can't you see how apprecia-tive she is of my time, and how you are interrupting us?"

Mr. Hemoglobin chuckled to himself. "This ain't a welfare mama. Where did you get her? Why are you keeping her from me? Who is she?!"

"Shut your filthy mouth Hubert. She most certainly is a welfare mother, and I am trying to change her life."

"She's one of our nieces, ain't she? Nothin wrong with that. Kissin cousins. Keep it in the family, you know? Must keep the blood pure. Come on honey. Want a shot of gin?"

"No she doesn't," cried Mrs. Hemoglobin. She sat up straight as a board in her chair. "Take your filthy self out of this room."

Mr. Hemoglobin swayed drunkenly and his eyes focused and unfocused on Tremble. "I used to sack girls like you all the time when I was young. Two and three at a time. That's when I was young and good-lookin. And when I still had money."

"Whatever do you mean, Hubert," said Mrs. Hemoglobin. Her voice wavered a little. "Of course you, I mean, we still have money."

Mr. Hemoglobin wobbled on his feet. "Mortgaged to the hilt!" he finally called out. "Not a dime to our names!" Then he looked at Tremble. "Speaking of to the hilt."

"Hubert," said Mrs. Hemoglobin, "let's not bore Miss White with our family history."

"Family history!" Mr. Hemoglobin yelled. "Blah! I'm talkin about money. We're poor as paupers. Even our termites are poor! All I can afford to do is sit up there and play with my sword all day. Not like the old days. Had all that family money. That Hemoglobin money. Money from civil-war profiteering, and then from the liquor trade. And now it's all gone. Gave it to the girls. Thinkin about going into the drug trade, me and Holmes here. That's where the quick bucks are nowadays. Never worked a day in my life, but maybe it's not too late to restore the Hemoglobin fortune. Whadda you say, Mr. Holmes?"

Holmes smiled and nodded. "No thank you, sir. I'm not a businessman."

Mrs. Hemoglobin let out a nervous, fake little laugh. "Now Hubert, Miss White and I have important matters to discuss. Please excuse us."

Mr. Hemoglobin leaned near Tremble. "Like my uniform?" he asked her. His awful breath reeked of gin. "The girls all liked to see me in uniform. Come on. I'll show you my medals. I'll show you my sword. Nobody's upstairs. We don't have any servants. Just this little kid that Alga has working for pennies, and he doesn't mind a free show."

Mrs. Hemoglobin nodded to Holmes, who disappeared into the kitchen.

Mr. Hemoglobin pulled out his sword and waved it in the air wildly. "I'll show you how I use this sword," he cried. "I'll show you how my great great grandfather cut down the Union soldiers left and right!" Mr. Hemoglobin let out a war-cry and started dashing at the curtains and slicing them apart.

He may have done considerable damage, but Holmes appeared with a gun. Holmes calmly aimed and fired at Mr. Hemoglobin. A blue dart hit Mr. Hemoglobin's rear, and he collapsed to the floor a moment later. Holmes then inserted a wheeled sled under Mr. Hemoglobin and dragged him out of sight.

"So," said Mrs. Hemoglobin cheerily. "Where were we?"

"A job," Tremble ventured.

"Oh yes, a job," said Mrs. Hemoglobin. "Let's see. Do you have any particular interests or talents?"

"I like to drink," said Tremble.

"Well, excellent—drinking. Let's think now. How

about a cocktail waitress? I think you'd be excellent at that job," Mrs. Hemoglobin declared

"Don't you have anything that involves, well, less work?"

"How much less did you have in mind?"

"None, actually," said Tremble.

"I'm afraid that's not an option, my dear mother," said Mrs. Hemoglobin. "I hate to do this to you, but I think I'll have to employ tough love. My report to the agency will recommend that we take you *off* welfare."

Mrs. Hemoglobin motioned Holmes over. He brought with him an old phone. Mrs. Hemoglobin cranked it and asked the operator for the Boosevelt Hotel.

"Yes, Mr. Upuras please. Donald?... Hello, this is Mrs. Hemoglobin.... Yes, yes, fine thank you.... And you?... Good, now I have a favor to ask you.... No, I don't need you to use extra rooms to house homeless people.... Yes, I do understand that they emptied the mini bars of all the liquor and urinated in the hallways last time.... No, Donald, I need you to put an acquaintance of mine to work as a cocktail waitress in your bar.... Why, yes, she does happen to be a welfare mother, but she is quite attractive.... No, I'm afraid housekeeper won't do—she'd probably steal too many things. I'm really determined that she be a cocktail waitress.... Drug test? Why that wouldn't be appropriate, now would it Donald?... Well I'm sure she's

on them, but she's kicking the habit.... Yes, we're empow-
ering her, don't you see?... No, Donald, I'm afraid the
drug test won't work.... I see, I see, yes, yes.... Is that the
way it is going to be then?...Oh, Donald, I'm so sorry to
hear that.... Why am I sorry? For pulling the Sisters of the
Confederacy annual ball out of your hotel, and blacklist-
ing the hotel on all charity functions.... Why yes, I'm
afraid it is necessary, Donald. Either you're with us or
against us.... Oh wonderful! I'm so glad you've come
around.... Send her over right away? That will be fine.
Thank you Donald. You won't be sorry." And with that
Mrs. Hemoglobin hung up the phone.

"There, there my dear girl," said Mrs. Hemoglobin.
"Isn't this exciting? Your first job."

And the funny thing was, it was to be Tremble's first
job.

Tremble experiences
the convenience of
public transportation

Mrs. Hemoglobin sent Tremble on her way to the
Boosevelt Hotel, which was downtown, near the French
district. Mrs. Hemoglobin gave Tremble enough money
for streetcar fare, but no more, and instructed Holmes to
stand with her at the streetcar stop and make sure she got

on. Mrs. Hemoglobin also instructed Tremble to watch out for all the "criminals, deviants and perverts" who lived in the French district, and were fond of wandering across Canal Street to drink in the hotel—and to take special care to avoid the even seedier people, "the artists, writers and grande dames."

As they waited, Tremble asked Holmes, "Are they really that poor?"

"Poorer than poor," said Holmes. "The poor have nothing. The Hemoglobins have less than nothing. They owe."

"Don't they have any children?"

Holmes shook his head and said dryly, "The Hemoglobin well has no more water in it."

"So why do you work for them? You seem to be a boy of some ability."

"Who else would hire a ten-year-old," said Holmes. "It's illegal. As soon as I can legally work I'm going to become a lawyer. That's where the money is these days. And then I'm going to get out of this town."

"Where to?" asked Tremble.

"The twentieth century," said Holmes.

"I see," said Tremble. "Oh, and please refrain from pinching me."

The streetcar came lumbering up the avenue with a cacophony of screeches and groans. Unfortunately, the

weather was nice, so the streetcar was packed with tourists. They had all stuffed themselves in. There must have
been two hundred people on the streetcar, judging from
the arms, legs, heads and other body parts sticking out the
windows. The streetcar came to a stop with an ear-splitting, animal-like howl appropriate for hell. It stood there
throbbing. The door slid open.

"Weh-ell, step on up," cried the driver. He was a cra-
zy-looking man with a big head of hair shoved under a
cap. The cap had a picture of Jesus on it. "Step aboard the
St. Withburga Streetcar, young woman. This ain't no
time for in-de-cision. This is time for gettin de vision, if
you know what I mean."

The driver turned around and started yelling at the
passengers in the foulest of terms. "Get back! Move back
all you stinkin, borin, jabberin tourists! Get on back, we
got a lady tryin to get on! That's right, a lady! Get on all
the way back to Wisconsin or Idaho or wherever you
from!"

The tourists made some effort to move, but they were
stuffed too tightly.

"Looks like I'm gonna have to get some assistance,"
said the driver. He reached above and pulled out a long
stick. "Say hello to my assistance." He started beating and
prodding the tourists with the stick. There was a lot of
yelling and screaming and commotion, and a few of the

tourists fell out of the windows. Finally the herd receded enough for Tremble to enter the car.

"Like cattle, like cattle I say," he said to Tremble. "If me 'n Jesus want to get 'em to move, you gotta move 'em all at once."

"Like Jesus?" said Tremble.

"Yeah, like Jee-ha-sus! Rides with me and looks out for me. Why he's sittin there right up on my cap. You blind, young lady? Now stand close to me 'n Jee-ha-sus and you won't get crushed."

The door slid shut and the streetcar started with a blood-curdling howl down the neutral ground of St. Withburga Avenue. It shook.

"Shake all you want, ol' buggy, but keep on a rollin'," sang the driver.

The streetcar rattled.

"Rattle all you want, ol' buggy, but keep on a rollin'," sang the driver.

The streetcar rolled on.

"Ah-ha-shake, rattle and roll! Yeh-has. Praise Jesus!" the driver hollered.

Just then, an ear-splitting "crack" was heard and a fireball shot out from under the car and incinerated a group of tourists waiting at a stop. Only scattered dentures, several pairs of blackened jogging shoes, and assorted smoldering fanny packs remained. The driver continued on slowly.

"Oh, nelly, look what you've done now," he said. "This buggy is a eighty year-old rolling electrical hazard. Would you use a hair dryer for eighty years?" he asked Tremble.

"Certainly not," said Tremble. "I can't imagine being eighty years old, with all the wrinkles. It must be awful."

"Yeah-has," sang out the driver. "You'd be electrocuted in a minute with an appliance that old."

The driver called in the incident on his radio.

"Are they all gone?" asked the dispatcher.

"Every last one of 'em, up in a puff of smoke. Gone to see Jee-sus," said the driver.

"Continue on. As long as you didn't hit a local."

The streetcar groaned and rocked from side to side as it pushed forward. The driver swung and manhandled several old metal handles and knobs.

Then all of the sudden the hooting and hollering of a large crowd was heard. A gang of young children rode up on bikes and jumped onto the moving streetcar, trying to strip off pieces of metal that could be pawned. The driver seemed well-used to these things. He rammed the knob to full speed, grabbed his assistance, and began to beat the kids who were hanging on the front of the car. "Get off— get off there! This here is public property! Get back in school. Nothin to get here! Don't make me send Jee-ha-sus after ya!"

The tourists were all screaming bloody murder of

course, and the driver called out, "Nobody touch any metal!" The driver pulled out two thick wires that were dangling near his feet and touched them together. A "bmmmf!" was heard as a terrific electrical shock shot through the car. The children hanging on the car shrieked and fell off. A group of German riders who didn't understand English found their hair and eyebrows burnt off and their zippers welded shut.

"Gets 'em every time," said the driver. "Don't see why they don't learn."

Up ahead they saw a dense growth.

"Oh lordy, now's the time to pray to Jee-sus." The driver crossed himself.

Tremble crossed herself as well. The mass of tourists looked around apprehensively. You see, the city's parks department had either been on strike, laid-off, on vacation, or sick for several decades, and so none of the grass in the public areas had been cut. Consequently, certain areas of the city, including several stretches of the St. Withburga Avenue neutral ground, had reverted to completely primitive, jungle-like growth.

"Looks like I'm gonna need assistance again," said the driver.

They barreled through grass ten feet high; through azaleas aflame with flowers gone mad; under oaks that threw their gnarled limbs up in the air and obscured all light; through banana trees and crepe myrtles and elephant ears and iron plants and palms and ferns and wisteria. A thick, steamy mist enveloped them.

The driver stuck his stick out the window and hacked and whacked at the vegetation. He cursed the devil and praised Jesus. The tourists pressed forward to see where they were going, for the windows had all become darkened and obscured by plants pressing close. The driver turned around and cursed the tourists and beat them back. In this fashion they continued for a few miles...

A steady drumbeat was heard, emanating from somewhere in the wilderness.

"What's that?" Tremble asked.

"War drums," said the driver.

"War drums?" said Tremble.

"The natives are a-risin up against the streetcars again. They defendin their territory against civilization, oh yeah-hass." Beads of sweat were coming down the deep ridges in the driver's face. "Man oh man I don't know how I do this every day." He wiped himself with a towel that had a picture of Jesus on it. "Ooh Jee-ha-sus," he began to sing. "Deliver me from this foreign land. Lead me through like you led Moses through the desert. Except let's do it in less than forty years."

Through dense underbrush Tremble saw clearings here and there where small fires smoked and smoldered, with squirrels and stray animals hanging above.

The drumbeats came steadier now, faceless, omnipresent, ominous. "Me 'n Jesus don't like the sound of that," said the driver. "The drums are saying that they are a-risin up." He nervously pushed the car to full speed.

Then a blood-curdling cry came from the natives hidden deep in the vegetation. The car was assailed with rocks and beads and old tin cans and bottles and other trash. The stuff came flying out of the jungle. The tourists at the windows complained very loudly. Once a few were dumped out in order to satisfy the lust of the natives, the assault ceased as quickly as it had begun.

"They really ought to cut that grass," said the driver. "Gets worse every year. Thank the lord for sending us plenty of tourists, though. Yeh-has. Thank you Jee-sus."

The streetcar came back to daylight and civilization. It rattled through downtown. The streets were walled high with the columns of granite banks and abandoned cotton and slave exchanges. They passed these old buildings, which were empty and begrimed like ruins. The once mighty firms they housed were long deceased. The only tenants were pigeons that loitered on the broken windows like stale memories.

The Boosevelt
shows Tremble
what service means

Tremble got out at the Boosevelt hotel. The whole idea of a job was disgusting, but she did find herself in front of a grand hotel. And grand hotels meant three things—beds, liquor, and wealthy men. Perhaps the three might be mixed together to produce a rich husband. So Tremble walked forward.

She went through the massive brass doors. She drifted through a cavernous lobby glittering with gold leaf and Belgian crystal chandeliers. Past antique grandfather clocks worth hundreds of thousands of dollars; priceless Oriental carpets and Louis XIV furniture; fields of marble on the floors and walls, much of it scavenged from demolished Parisian buildings.

Tremble was drifting around the hotel in her muumuu when she felt someone firmly grab her arm. It was a bellhop. He pulled her to a desk that once belonged to a Prussian king.

"Got one," chirped the bellhop.

The man behind the desk, the assistant general manager, lowered his glasses and considered Tremble. "One of Mrs. Hemoglobin's projects—Miss White, I presume," he sniffed. "Very well, just don't let her near the liquor."

"There's been a mistake," Tremble whined.

"Oh I'm sure there has been," said the man without looking up. "Yours was a little over twenty years ago, I'm supposing."

The man finished writing something on an official piece of Boosevelt hotel stationary and handed it to the bellhop. The bellhop put it into a pneumatic tube. "Whoop" and away it went.

A few minutes later there was another "whoop" and a message appeared at the tube.

"What does it say?" asked the assistant general manager.

The bellhop turned the note this way and that and finally said, "I can't read, sir, that's why I'm still a bellhop."

"Give it here," said the assistant general manager. "It says to take her to Mr. Upuras."

"Upuras?" the bellhop repeated, fearfully.

"Upuras!" The assistant general manager pounded his fist on the desk. "Immediately!"

The bellhop composed himself. "This way, ma'am."

Tremble was dragged under the chandeliers, past the gilded columns, around huge bouquets of tropical flowers flown in daily from the rain forests. A harpist sent her magical notes through the lofty rooms—rooms fit for royalty. They went through grand doors fifteen feet high. Legions of workers were polishing the brass, shining the mirrors, dusting the furniture—light was everywhere, shining from every surface. "How are you, sir? How are you, madam? Enjoying your stay?" the workers asked every guest in sight.

Then Tremble and the bellhop approached a little door. It was hardly five feet high and almost imperceptible. The bellhop pulled Tremble into a dank little hall, which led down into an even danker little tunnel. Naked bulbs hung overhead. Great twisting bunches of pipes and wires covered the ceiling. The hotel's inner organs let loose a weird hum. Hotel workers pushed by, bitching and groaning and sweating. The ceiling got lower. Tremble and the bellhop had to stoop down.

They turned to a small, windowless office, barely five feet wide and five feet high. There they beheld the general manager of the grand Boosevelt hotel, Mr. Upuras, hard at work.

He was a short, clean man in his 60s wearing a natty suit and bow tie. He looked up and nervously adjusted his spectacles.

"I thought you were to bring me the welfare mama," he said, in a high, chatty little voice.

"This is Miss White," said the bellhop.

"I can see that," snapped Mr. Upuras. "Oh, dear. I am

really very disappointed. I had hoped for something better from Mrs. Hemoglobin. Come on in if you must."

Tremble was pushed into the claustrophobic little room and the door shut behind her. "Sit right there," said Mr. Upuras, motioning to a marble bust of George Washington.

Mr. Upuras looked at a chart on the wall and shook his head worriedly. "I'll never meet these hiring goals, never."

Just then there was a "whoop" and a round container appeared in the pneumatic tube. Mr. Upuras pulled out a piece of paper. After reading it he began to wring his small hands. "Another boycott, oh dear, oh dear. I'm afraid we're on all of their shit lists now, excuse my French."

Mr. Upuras wrung his hands even more, until his knuckles were white. "It wasn't like this when I started. Now, the *customer is always right*. But look at our customers! Tank tops and flip flops. And everyone complaining. I had to take this original bust of George Washington out of the lobby because of the complaints. And now he is a chair. Everyone sits on his head. What a horrible fate. I had to move to this windowless office because the windows were becoming too tempting."

The little man contemplated this for a moment, and then brightened slightly.

"But every now and then something happens that

reminds me of the grand old days. This morning, for instance, I just hired a new bartender. One of the best hires I have ever made. He bartended at the Carlyle. You, my dear, will have the pleasure of working with him. See if you can learn a thing or two. See if you can make this old relic happy."

"George Washington?" said Tremble.

"No, me, you foolish girl," said Mr. Upuras, turning cross suddenly. He pressed a button on his desk and immediately a woman in a white uniform appeared. "She's to be a cocktail waitress," said Mr. Upuras. "You know what to do with her, Mrs. Binding, so do what needs to be done."

Mrs. Binding looked Tremble over. "She's worse than most of them," she grunted. "A muumuu, of all things. How disrespectful of the Boosevelt."

Tremble was whisked away to a room where maids were crawling in and out. She was quickly stripped and hosed down. Then they put her through a delousing treatment and hosed her down again, before dressing her in a black skirt, white shirt and bow tie.

Tremble felt like dying. It really was horrible—the uniform and all. She suspected it had polyester in it. She even cried a little when nobody was looking, and she needed a drink in the worst way.

"Stop sniffling!" cried Mrs. Binding.

Tremble was pulled to a small windowless training room, where she was forced to watch films on customer service that told her over and over that one must listen to the customer, and the customer was always right, no matter how obnoxious, ignorant, or boring that customer might be.

Then she was expelled from the hotel's bowels, out to the glitter of the ballrooms and salons. She felt like a prisoner in her itchy uniform. They were leading her to the famed Boosevelt Lounge. She and Ennui once drank there in high style, before that unfortunate incident when Ennui tied a large women's dress to the piano, resulting in an entertaining display of public nudity.

Mr. Upuras himself appeared and led her into the lounge. The other cocktail waitress was there. Her name was Bernadetta, and she had been at the Boosevelt for over fifty years.

"Bernadetta, impart your years of wisdom into this young soul," said Mr. Upuras, sticking his finger high into the air. "She's uneducated, and is used to living on welfare and smoking crack. So assume that she knows nothing. Teach her the grand ways of Boosevelt tradition," he said proudly.

Bernadetta rubbed her spectacles and addressed a marble column. "I'll do my best, sir," she croaked.

Mr. Upuras vanished. He had business to attend to.

Apparently there was a demonstration being held outside. It was a protest of the hotel's high rates, which caused discrimination against the poor.

Tremble stood there in her silly uniform, not knowing what to do. "Where can I get a drink?" she asked Bernadetta.

"Is somebody talking to me?" Bernadetta asked. She looked around, but could see no one. So she sat on a large Rococo couch and dozed off.

Tremble tapped her on the shoulder. "I said, where can I get a drink, for example, a martini?"

"What, huh," said Bernadetta, waking suddenly. "Who is it? You a customer? If you want a drink, go to the bartender. He's behind the flowers. I've been cocktailing for over fifty years. I once served Truman a beer. I used to have real teeth." Then she fell back asleep.

Tremble shrugged. The lounge was empty for the moment. She went to the bar. It was a marble thing from an aristocrat's estate that was burned during the French Revolution. The stain from where the owner's body had burned was still etched into the surface.

"Yes ma'am," said the bartender.

"Ennui!" yelled Tremble.

"I'm sorry," said the bartender. "My name is Larry. And you must be mistaken."

Tremble practices her customer service skills

"Ennui!" Tremble positively begged. "How did you get here?"

"My name isn't Ennui, miss, it is Larry. And I got here by plane, which I took from New York, where I used to work."

"Oh, Ennui. I don't care how you got here. I've had the most horrible time since you left. Social workers, religious education, tourists, public transportation—you were right. We should have fled the country."

"My Boosevelt nametag clearly says Larry," said the bartender. "And if you'll excuse me, I have some glasses to polish. If you are the new cocktail waitress, I would advise you to begin straightening and wiping down the tables. Our evening guests will arrive soon. And be sure to move Bernadetta. She tends to take the best seats."

"Oh, Ennui, please fix me a martini. I've been dying for one. You won't believe what I've been through. It's like I'm in a nightmare and I can't wake up," Tremble cried.

"Perhaps you *are* in a nightmare," said the bartender. "And as for a martini, certainly not. Employees are not allowed to drink on the job."

"But you're sipping a martini," Tremble whined.

"I told you I had some glasses to polish off. I'm merely testing product quality. Boosevelt guests demand the very best."

The bartender tossed a wet rag at Tremble. "Wipe down some tables, and perhaps I'll let you test product quality as well," he said.

Tremble took the rag off her head and stared at it. "Aren't there janitors to do this?"

Just then an elderly couple came in and sat down at a table. The man was stooped and coughed disgustingly. The old lady clapped her hands and waived at Tremble. "Miss, miss!" she called.

"Why is that lady yelling at me?" Tremble sniffed. "She acts like she knows me."

"You are supposed to go over to her," said the bartender as he adjusted his bow-tie and black vest. "That is what a cocktail waitress does."

"And then what do I do?" asked Tremble.

"You are supposed to ask what they want, then get it," said the bartender.

"Oh yes, Ennui, that's right. The customer is always right. They took me to this room and tried to brainwash me with these movies. It was awful."

"My name is Larry," said the bartender again. "And we have customers waiting."

Tremble stomped her foot and pouted. The bartender paid no attention to her. He was too busy mixing himself another martini. Tremble went to the couple. "Is that your husband?" she asked.

"Why, yes," said the old lady in a quivering voice.

"Well, please ask him to stop coughing. It's disturbing the other customers."

Then Tremble stomped back to the bar.

"What did they want?" asked the bartender.

"How would I know?" said Tremble. "Like I care. Please."

"Well go back and find out," said the bartender. "Your customer service skills are quite vomitous."

"Quit being such an ass," said Tremble.

The man was coughing even more violently. Tremble went over.

"Miss," said the old lady. "Could you please bring my husband some water? He needs to take his pills."

Tremble went back. "Did they say what they wanted?" said the bartender.

"I don't know," said Tremble. She slumped over the bar and put her hand to her head. "It's been so awful, Ennui. Let's get out of here and go drinking. I tried to play the martyr, but it just didn't fit me. I tried to reform my life—I really did. But it didn't work. It was like an outfit that was too tight and itchy."

A group of tourists came in and sat down. After they finished admiring the furnishings through a series of infantile noises, they got impatient. At the restaurants at home, the waitress always approaches right away. What was the matter with this place?

After they yelled and motioned for a while, Tremble was sufficiently annoyed to approach them.

"Yes," said Tremble.

"Can we have some drinks," said a man.

"Do you have money?" Tremble replied curtly.

"Well of course we have money," blubbered the man.

"You don't look like it, judging from your awful outfits. I don't know what you were thinking. I've never seen anything so cheap or in such bad taste. Suspenders, worn without a coat. How vomitous."

"Vomitous?" said the man.

He got up to slap Tremble, but one of the women, who was smiling desperately, grabbed his hand and pulled him down. "Now Arnie, we said we were going to have fun this vacation, remember. We've spent all this money on this vacation and goodness gracious we are going to have fun," she hissed.

She turned to Tremble. "Young lady, we've come all the way from Michigan. And we would love a mint julep. We're told that's what people drink here."

"Yech," said Tremble. "Have you ever had one?

They're disgusting. I think the people who used to drink them have died off by now."

"How about a gin fizz?"

Tremble crossed her eyes and stuck out her tongue.

"A Sazerac?"

Tremble put her finger down her throat and pretended to throw up.

"Well, we'd like to have two of each," said the lady. "We'll try them ourselves."

"Are you sure you are in the right city?" Tremble asked. "I am telling you, nobody drinks those nasty things here."

The lady pulled out a brochure and waved it in Tremble's face. "It says right here that these are the famous drinks of this city. So we *have* to have them."

"As you wish," said Tremble. She stood there without moving. The tourists looked at her, confused.

"Aren't you going to pay me?" Tremble asked.

The man got up again like he was going to slap Tremble, but the woman yanked him down with a ferocious pull. She took $100 out of her purse. "Just bring us the change."

Tremble walked to the bar. She fingered the money. Maybe cocktail waitressing wasn't so bad.

"What did they want?" said the bartender, who was finishing off a martini.

"Just a bunch of stupid tourist drinks. Who cares. Make me a martini."

"What did I say about employees drinking?"

"Well, I just quit," said Tremble. "I'll pay you for a martini. I have some money now."

"Go take care of some of those other customers, and I'll think about it," said the bartender. "Go on, get out there. Mush mush."

Tremble stomped her foot and pouted and walked back out into the lounge.

A man who looked vaguely familiar walked in and sat down. He was wearing a gray suit and had a briefcase by his side.

Tremble stumbled like she was looking at a ghost. She shook her head. She pulled at her hair. She rubbed her eyes. "James Potts!" she cried. "Aren't you dead?"

"Well, yes, I was," said Mr. Potts. "And you are—the martini girl."

"But what are you doing alive?"

"I'm suing the ambulance company. What else would I be doing? I should get at least three hundred million for a wrongful death suit. And for once I'll get the full benefit of my hard work, not the client, who in almost all cases just happened to get lucky by being maimed by a car or poisoned by a chemical plant or what have you."

"But how?"

"How? The ambulance company was none other than Healthbomb, which happens to be the largest, wealthiest medical company in the world—although it will probably be the second-largest by the time I am done with them."

"I saw you squished with my own eyes!"

"That's absolutely right. But I already have enough witnesses, plus the coroner's report to prove that I was killed by a Healthbomb ambulance. Would you mind getting me a drink? How about a rusty nail? That would really hit the spot."

Tremble scampered back to the bar. "Ennui, make me a rusty nail. Quick! I have to get this customer really drunk because he's rich."

The bartender turned around and leveled a boorish gaze at Tremble. "So be it," he said. He mixed this and that and shook a shaker and produced a martini.

"That's not a rusty nail."

"That's all I know how to make," said the bartender. "If he doesn't like it I'll make him another."

Tremble shrugged and brought the drink to James Potts. On the way, the old lady cried "Miss!", the old man coughed disgustingly, and the tourists waved their hands impatiently.

Tremble stuck her nose in the air and ignored them.

"This isn't what I ordered," said Mr. Potts.

Tremble slid next to him on the sofa. "Pardon?"

"Never mind," said Mr. Potts. He raised the martini to his lips and sipped it. "Excellent martini, though."

Tremble stared into his eyes and smiled. "Weren't you going to make me rich?"

"Oh, that. I think I did say that. I had just finished smoking crack at the time, so I'm not sure. But in any case I'm not taking any more cases. This one is it. After this, I'm retiring to my own private island in the Caribbean. It can be like heaven there. I've been in this racket for too long. I'm thirty-three, and so forth."

Tremble's chest heaved in excitement. She would have heaved herself onto James Potts, but there was all sorts of uproar in the bar. The old lady marched up to Tremble and cried that she was going to see the manager about her. The old man hacked like his insides were about to come out. The tourists were braying like asses. Perhaps she would have to serve them.

"Excuse me," she said to Mr. Potts. She stomped back to the bartender. "Make me seven drinks," she said. The bartender shook a lot of things and poured and mixed and produced seven martinis.

Tremble dropped off six of them to the tourists, and one to the old man. His wife had left him to go see the manager. The old man had stopped coughing. In fact, he had stopped moving, blinking and breathing as well. He sat there wide-eyed and stiff as a board.

Tremble felt for his pulse. "I seem to have quite a number of people dying these days," she thought to herself. "But they usually come back to life. In any case, he must pay for his drink." She reached into his coat pocket and pulled out his wallet. It was stuffed with hundreds. She took the money and a credit card. "This ought to do," she thought. "The Boosevelt is quite expensive, you know."

Then she went back to the bar. The tourist lady was waiting for her. "You again?" Tremble groaned.

"These aren't the drinks we asked for."

"Yes they are," said Tremble.

"No they are not," said the lady. "These are all the same, and we asked for three different drinks."

"Madam, what were the drinks you needed?" asked the bartender, who appeared to be drunk.

The lady told him. "We'll bring them over right away," he said.

The bartender then made another batch of martinis, which he proceeded to drink.

Tremble sat down by Mr. Potts and tried to talk to him but there was a riot in the lounge. There were more and more upset tourists. Dozens of other tables had been filled and people were snapping their fingers and clapping their hands and screaming "miss—waitress—my god what is wrong with this place!" The bartender was napping on the impression of the scorched nobleman.

Tremble tried to ignore the customers but they began to gather big bouquets of flowers. They doused them in martinis and lit them with the candles that were on the tables. They began to gather together and make violent noises.

As this was occurring, a man wearing a smoking jacket, cuff links, slacks and tasseled loafers sauntered in.

The bartender awoke with a shot and ran towards him.

The man saw the crowd and burning torches. He cried "lynch mob!" and fled.

Tremble jumped into the arms of Mr. Potts. "Save me," she cried.

They all ran for their lives. They ran under the chandeliers. They ran past grand columns. They ran past Mr. Upuras. They ran through the brass doors. "Have a good evening," said the doorman, who subtly extended his hand for a tip.

Mr. Potts provides a satisfying meal

Fabulo jumped into a black Cadillac parked on the street and drove off, country music blaring. Tremble and James Potts got into a limousine. The bartender entered as well.

"Follow that Cadillac!" screamed Larry.

The limousine squealed off, bounding over the pot-holed streets. They found, though, that they had jumped into the wrong car.

"This isn't my limo," said James Potts. "Sorry about this," he said to the people who were sitting in it.

"That's okay, honey," said a hardened old lady who was smoking two cigarettes at once. "You want a draft?"

There was a small bar in the limousine, complete with a beer tap. Several old men were lined up on a sofa, smoking and drinking slowly.

"No offense, but I only drink bottled beer," said James Potts. "It's more sanitary."

"Hey guys, you hear that? He only drinks bottled beer," the lady crowed.

All the old men cackled and slapped each other on the back and repeated what she had said.

"Well that's what he's going to get, then," said the lady. The men shut up and went back to leaning over their beers. The lady reached into a cooler and pulled out a Jax.

"Pardon me," said Larry, "don't you own a bar? I can't remember the name."

"I could never remember the name either, honey," she replied. "But yeah, I was there. Bartended there for thirty years. Then some customer gave me a tip on a stock that was about to go into the crapper. I sold it short and made twenty million."

Tremble stomped her foot and pouted. "How come everybody around here is rich but me? It just isn't fair," she said. "Nobody can spend money as well as I do, and therefore it makes sense that I should have plenty of it."

The lady shrugged. She pulled another round of drafts for everyone and lit up more cigarettes. Then she put a coin in a jukebox and a sad song came on. A neon beer sign glowed behind her.

The driver turned around and said, "I think the car is heading for the zoo, ma'am."

"Must be another one of those animal traffickers," said Mr. Potts. "That's all the rage now, to have exotic pets. Everyone has pure-bred dogs and cats these days, and that's not enough. Why, one of my girlfriends wanted a tiger of all things—a pet tiger! She saw one on television and thought it would be cute. There are people who can get these sorts of things for you. Black market and what have you."

"And what happened?" asked Tremble.

"It ate her, of course. I tried to tell her, but once she got an idea in her head, you couldn't get it out."

"How horrid," Tremble sighed. She inched closer to Mr. Potts and put her hand on his most important leg.

"Actually not," he said. "She was losing her looks, and as a result her conversation was no longer interesting."

Larry finished his beer. "Well, I believe that we should get on with things. I have clothes to recover. And things seem to be lagging."

"That's right," said Mr. Potts. "Recovering clothes is a real point of honor."

They had been driving at a high rate of speed, flying along the city's various grand, mansion-lined avenues and squalid, shack-crowded alleys. The limousine came to a halt and the song came to an end. Larry slowly opened the door. There was quietness and shadowy darkness all around them. They were in a vast, lush park of huge oaks, shimmering lagoons and fragrant fields of moonlit grass. Larry got out. Tremble followed, and James Potts as well.

"Come again," said the lady. The limousine slid off into the night.

They saw the Cadillac parked underneath a cove of crepe myrtles. It was empty.

"Look," said Tremble. "You've got your Cadillac. Now let's go."

"Not quite," said Larry. "I need to recover my jacket, loafers, slacks and cuff links."

"Ennui, this is enough," said Tremble. "I am not about to go sneaking off into that zoo trying to find this man just to recover clothing."

"For the last time I am not Ennui," said Larry. "And I need this clothing, because without it I will never be able to marry my sweetheart."

"I am your sweetheart," cried Tremble. "And I don't give a darn about your clothing, or anything else."

"I'm afraid you are mistaken," said Larry. "My sweetheart is nothing like you. As though I would be with someone who would so quickly embrace and abandon human emotion, as though it were a pair of shoes."

Tremble was about to reply, but Larry had already headed off into the park, towards the zoo. His dark image danced underneath the huge hall of oaks that led to the entrance. Through the leaves breezes swept and moonlight flitted. It was all very haunting.

"Drat, he makes me so mad," said Tremble. "Let's leave. This is creepy."

But Mr. Potts did not want to leave, as his resolve had hardened. "Actually, let's go look around the zoo a bit. I'm curious to see what this boy is up to."

They walked forward and saw Larry scramble over the old iron fence. They followed suit. "Oh darnit," said Tremble. "I ripped my clothing."

"I see that," said Mr. Potts.

Tremble frowned and they continued following Larry. They could see his shadowy form skipping along the arcade of a replicated Palladian villa that housed the aquarium. They followed him to the old field of ancient oaks—trees with huge trunks and gnarled limbs that completely obscured the sky. They saw him dancing through the antiquated fountain. The statue of the maiden looked down silently upon him. She was holding a jug that poured water into the mouth of a bronze boy. Larry put his mouth to the water and drank. Then he began to splash around. Granite frogs surrounded the fountain, spitting out streams. Their eyes were fixed and calm.

It was so dark, now, under the trees. The moon's light only penetrated in brief splashes. Larry ran on towards the replica of a Greek temple that held the sea lions. James Potts and Tremble followed. Larry jumped in and splashed in the water. The sea lions made barking and belching sounds around him. Their oily black bodies slid in and out of the water.

"He's gone mad," said Tremble. "He must be drunk out of his mind."

The zoo was once again eerily quiet. There were no sounds of the animals. They heard Larry's footsteps as he ran off to the swamp exhibit. James Potts and Tremble continued walking and found themselves on a wooden footbridge over a recreated swamp. Alligators slept on the banks of the muddy water. Turtles sat on logs. Thick bamboo crowded around all the edges. The sky was visible here, and the stars twinkled delicately.

"We should take a rest," said Mr. Potts. "This is a nice spot, with a great view of the sky."

Mr. Potts put down his briefcase and sat on it. Tremble sat on the edge of the bridge and dangled her legs over the water. They looked up to the heavens.

"Have you ever made a wish upon a star?" asked Mr. Potts.

"What? Oh, you mean have I ever wished I looked like a star? All the time. But not an old star."

"No, you don't know what I mean. Look for a falling star."

They looked up to the sky again. "I don't see anything," said Tremble after a few seconds. "This is boring."

Right then a flash lit up the sky as a star streaked across it.

"Now make a wish," said Mr. Potts.

Tremble closed her eyes.

"What did you wish?" he asked a minute later.

"I wished that I was rich," said Tremble, with her eyes still tightly shut. "I live in a big mansion with plenty of servants and a car to take me wherever I want to go."

"Let me tell you, from one who has a mansion with plenty of servants, that it's a big headache."

"What did you wish for?" asked Tremble, turning to James Potts, and batting her eyelids.

"I'll show you, and what have you," said Mr. Potts...

The apes were awakened from their sleep by a sound that touched the depths of their ancient, primal souls. Man and ape united in crying to the heavens, crying to an act as old as god—that of creation.

"Ooh, ooh, ooh, ahhh," cried Mr. Potts.

"Ooh, ooh, ooh, ooh," responded the apes. Their sounds echoed across the quiet city.

"Ah ah ah ah ah!" screamed the monkeys, who jumped up and down wildly.

"Ooh ah ooh ah ooh ah ooh," cried Mr. Potts, with increasing rapidity. "Oohoohooohooh!" He was flopping up and down so fast and with such energy that he suddenly flopped off the bridge and into the water.

"Eeeek!" said Tremble. She got up and peered into the murky depths. "Are you all right?"

"Of course I'm all right," Mr. Potts replied, treading water. The alligators slid off the banks. "I'm an attorney, and a plaintiff's attorney at that. I make thirty million a year. I have ten cars and four houses. I can sue the government. I can sue the police. I can sue anybody. I'm invincible!"

But Mr. Potts' words were now bubbles, as the reptiles dragged him deep into the water and stuffed him under an old log at the bottom of the pond. They would let the meat sit there for a few days so that it would get good and tender, and thus be more tasty.

Fabulo and Larry
discuss business

Tremble straightened up and found herself alone.
"That James Potts certainly is accident prone," she
thought. She wandered out of the swamp exhibit and
entered the primate area, which was fashioned as a walk
through a Central American jungle. She walked along
densely vegetated paths where ruins of Mayan temples
were meticulously reconstructed as the homes of monkeys and apes.

And there she saw Larry politely conversing with the
man wearing the smoking jacket. They were standing in
front of a temple that housed the apes. It was hard to see,
though, because the clouds had obscured the moon and
the night was pitch black.

"So what you are saying," said Larry, "is that people
will actually pay thousands of dollars to have these animals as pets. Very interesting indeed."

"Yeah," said Fabulo. "I'm taking inventory right now.
This stuff should be worth about fifteen million."

"But how will you capture and transport these animals?"

"That's the easy part," said Fabulo. "Zoo's been privatized. They laid off all the security."

"Excuse me," said Tremble. "Can we go now? I really have to pee."

"Please, we're discussing business," said Larry. He turned back to Fabulo. "Now, what kind of markup do you think you can make per animal? I find this very interesting. My father was a captain of industry, you see."

Tremble stomped her foot. She really had to go. It was very dark, but she thought she spotted a door nearby leading to a bathroom. She went through it.

"The rhinos will go for big bucks, because people want the biggest things," said Fabulo. "Big house, big car, big pet."

"What is that racket?" Larry asked, looking around.

They turned to see the faint image of an ape hoisting Tremble into the air. She was screaming bloody murder.

"Oh goodness," said Larry. "Young miss, please quit doing Jane imitations, will you? I am anything but king of the beasts, and I really don't feel like swinging on a vine to rescue you."

The ape tucked Tremble under one arm and ran around in circles, beating his chest the whole time.

"This'll bust up everything," said Fabulo. "If some girl gets killed by an ape I'll never sell this junk. Man, she needs to get out."

Fabulo disappeared through the door, and Larry could see his image chasing the ape. The moon suddenly came out from behind the clouds and glinted on one of Fabulo's cuff links. The ape immediately dropped Tremble. Then it grabbed Fabulo and began to rip the clothes from him. Several other apes were attracted by the cuff links glinting off the moon. They all fought for the clothing.

"Oh, the horror, the horror!" Larry cried. "My jacket may be ripped." Tremble came running out of the door. She was disheveled and her clothes were hanging on by a thread. She fell into Larry's water-soaked arms. "Ennui," she gasped.

"I'm sorry, my name is Larry," came the reply. And then fortune was kind to Tremble, covering her eyes with blackness and painting darkness over her mind.

They see
friends
at the zoo

Tremble awoke with a start. "Larry!" she shrieked.

Ennui was sleeping in a gilded chair. He held an empty martini glass perfectly upright in his hand.

His eyes crept open. "Please, no screaming," he replied. "Not before my morning martini of course. And please address me by my name, which is Ennui. I don't enjoy hearing the name of some boy you undoubtedly bestowed your favors upon."

"Oh Ennui, your name was Larry, and everything was horrible! First the social worker people got me and they tried to reform me," Tremble cried.

Ennui yawned and rose. He shook a shaker. "Haven't you noticed how dreams make the dullest stories when you tell them to others?"

"But it wasn't a dream, Ennui. It was real. I swear. Your name was Larry."

"Now why would my name be Larry," said Ennui. "That is truly ridiculous. My name is Ennui."

"No, you were Larry. And we were working at the Boosevelt Hotel."

"Ha!" Ennui laughed. "What nonsense." He walked to Tremble and gave her a martini, which she gladly drank. "They would never let me in there again after that lady streaked through the halls," said Ennui. "It was quite rude of her. I don't know why they were so mad at me."

"But we were there. You were a bartender, and I was the cocktail waitress. And the customers were trying to kill us. And James Potts rescued us," said Tremble.

"James Potts," said Ennui. "Isn't he dead?"

"No, he wasn't dead. Well, I mean he was dead because he is suing the ambulance company."

"Typical," Ennui sniffed.

"And then we chased Fabulo to the park because you wanted your things back. And then James Potts fell into the water and was eaten by alligators. It was all so real, Ennui."

"It sounds like it," said Ennui. He rolled his eyes. "I'm afraid the gin is beginning to rot your brain. I may have to cut you back. I don't think you have the proper constitution."

"And then I tried to pee in the ape exhibit, and an ape picked me up and started tossing me around. And I swear it felt like it was Bertel. And then Fabulo came in and all the apes started ripping his clothes off. I mean, your clothes off, because he was wearing your clothes."

"Have you finished yet," said Ennui. "We have a whole afternoon to plan, and we haven't even started thinking about it. What are we doing today?"

Tremble jumped out of bed and pulled on the nearest outfit. It was her black Chanel suit.

"Didn't you just wear that?" Ennui asked.

"Oh shut up, Ennui," Tremble replied. "You're starting to get on my nerves already. We're going to the zoo."

Ennui let out a laugh that sounded like a pig snort. "Please. The zoo? Where am I to find a well-mixed martini at the zoo? I'll have to drink beer. And beer is just so pedestrian."

"We are going to the zoo," Tremble cried as her hair went up. "And I am going to prove to you that I wasn't dreaming."

"And deal with all those brats running around and screaming? How vomitous. I'm afraid it just won't do. The zoo is for those people who come from the suburbs with their pig-snouted children."

Tremble stomped her foot. Ennui frowned and followed her out the door. They walked for a couple of miles through the city's rotting neighborhoods and made it to the park.

"Look," Tremble cried. "Car tracks. Right there. Under the crepe myrtle. That's where the Cadillac was."

"That doesn't prove anything," said Ennui.

They walked a bit more under the canopy of oaks and made it to the zoo.

"That will be fifty dollars," said the lady at the entrance gate.

"That's rather steep," said Ennui. "Doesn't she get a student discount?"

The lady eyed Tremble. "That'll be sixty, then. Students cost extra. Actually it's seventy now, because you asked me a question and took more time."

Ennui gave her the eye. "I'm sorry, we've privatized," the lady grunted. "Plus we have to cover the costs of the lawsuit over that whole Intesti mess."

Ennui reached into his pocket and pulled out the money.

"How did you get that money?" Tremble demanded.

"I'm not so poor as you think," said Ennui.

"You earned it from tips, right?"

"Oh, yes, when I was bartending. Please."

They walked a bit more. The zoo was, well, a zoo. It was a Saturday, you see, and thousands of double-income parents had dragged their children outside.

The children, who had spent the majority of their lives without parental supervision, growing up in the wilds of television, ran freely like beasts of the land.

They jumped up on railings. They attacked the fast food restaurants that the zoo had allowed within its doors. They stuffed cheeseburgers and french fries and ice cream through their smacking lips. They climbed all over the noble statue of Audubon, pummeling his nose and ears. They found the graceful statue of the goddess Diana, made fun of her exposed breasts, and humped her in imitation of things they had seen. They peed in the zoo's various grand fountains, and fought with each other over the coins beneath the water.

And they tormented the animals. Tremble and Ennui walked through the land of cats. A poor lion was lying in its exhibit, which was fashioned as a lonely cliff. It hardly moved its great head or enormous paws.

"Hey, you stupid cat," a kid was screaming. "Do something stupid cat—whatever your name is!" The kid pelted the cat with an empty french fry container. The cat looked up, and then put its head down.

Tremble and Ennui walked to the parrot exhibit. A colorful parrot was sitting on a tree.

Tremble looked at it. "Slut slut slut," the parrot squawked.

"How dare that parrot!" Tremble cried, turning pale. A bunch of children around them started to laugh.

Ennui almost collapsed in giggles. Then the parrot said, "Cheap cheap cheap cheap."

Ennui reddened and said crossly, "I think that's highly inappropriate. If these animals knew how much we paid to see them, surely they'd treat us better."

They walked by the elephant castle, which was a turreted structure where the elephants lived. The elephants lumbered in and out of a large door. An elephant trainer was making them lock the door behind them. Then the trainer made them do all sorts of stupid tricks, like sitting down and standing up. A few kids yawned and moved on.

"Why don't those elephants just pick up the trainers and kill them?" Ennui asked. "I would never allow myself to be imprisoned."

"Ennui, you don't know anything," said Tremble. "Those elephants have obviously committed some sort of terrible crime, and have therefore been imprisoned. They'll never be paroled except for good behavior."

"All the same," said Ennui. "I think it's too much to hang advertisements on the elephants. Privatization or no privatization, there's something strange about seeing a hamburger advertised on an animal."

"I really don't know what you mean, Ennui," Tremble replied.

Then they went on to look at other animals. They saw a babirusa, which was a wild hog from Indonesia, otherwise known as a pig deer. It ran around in circles and dug into the dirt with its tusks. They saw some monkeys known as black howlers.

"Look," said Tremble. "It says here that the black howlers repel intruders with their collective screaming"

"Sounds like attorneys," Ennui sniffed.

"Don't tell me you are still jealous of James Potts," said Tremble. "I already told you he was eaten by alligators. Isn't that punishment enough?"

"You only dreamed that he was eaten," said Ennui.

Tremble led him to the swamp exhibit. They walked out over the small replica of a swamp. Sure enough, there was James Potts' bloated body on the far shore, being mightily enjoyed by several snapping, masticating alligators. His meat had been properly cured and tenderized by this time.

"See," said Tremble. "I told you I wasn't dreaming."

"That doesn't prove anything," said Ennui. "His body

was obviously put to good use after the ambulance ran him over. He probably tried to sell his body to science but it was judged too disgusting a specimen for medical students to touch. Look how repulsive he is. I can't believe you were attracted to him."

"He's been rotting for at least a day or two," said Tremble in a huff. She grabbed Ennui's arm and led him into the depths of the primate exhibit. "I'm going to prove to you that I wasn't dreaming."

They went up to the temple of the apes. There they saw a dashing young ape sitting with his legs elegantly crossed. He was wearing the smoking jacket, the shirt with the shiny cuff links, the slacks and tasseled loafers.

"See," said Tremble. "Now explain that one."

"How dare an ape wear my clothing!" Ennui shrieked. "What is this world coming to?"

"He looks rather handsome," said Tremble. "The clothes fancy him much better than they do you."

It was one of those rare times that Ennui was about to explode in rage. He was so mad he could hardly talk.

"And look," said Tremble. "I told you that I thought it was Bertel who was manhandling me. There he is over there chewing on a tree limb. He's the one the apes are picking the bugs from. Toodles Bertel! How are you?"

Bertel looked up and grunted. He didn't seem to recognize them. There were always dozens of people scream-

ing for his attention, for a sign had been recently attached
to the ape exhibit, pointing out the special attraction of
this "killer ape." It had been fingerprinted and positively
identified as the murderer of Chef Intesti. A gang of children stood around and stared wide-eyed at this ferocious
animal.

More youngsters were starting to pour into the primate area. They jumped up and down and imitated the
animals, scratching under their arms and hooting and hollering. Then the primates got excited and jumped up and
down and imitated the children. The screaming got going
to a feverish pitch, with a cacophony of wild noises and
flailing limbs. It was difficult to tell the animals from the
people.

"I'm going to get my clothing," said Ennui.

"Don't," said Tremble. "Those apes will tear you apart.
Or worse, if they touch you, you'll smell like a stinky
ape."

"I don't care," said Ennui. He went forward, opened
the door and disappeared behind it. He appeared in the
temple a moment later. He approached the ape and pulled
out a fat wad of cash. Some negotiations took place, with
the ape getting the better of the bargain.

Ennui sauntered out, sporting his smoking jacket, cuff
links, slacks, and tasseled loafers.

"How about that?" Ennui said grandly.

"You stink," said Tremble, holding her nose. She was about to ask him something, but noticed that Ennui had left the door open.

Several apes came running out. The children saw the apes and everything became a panic of shrieks. The apes ran around, opening the monkey cages. The orangutans and chimpanzees and spider monkeys and black howlers and dozens of other primates poured out. They swung from branches and stole the ice cream and hamburgers and hot dogs from the hands of crying children.

Ennui yawned. "Goodness, how cliché," he said.

"How right you are," said Tremble. "And the noise is getting bothersome. Perhaps we should walk out to the river."

They go
to the river

They left the zoo, leaving the riot of beasts, as well as the animals, behind them. They approached old man river. It stretched peacefully by in a muddy, wide curve lined by cypress trees.

A strange expression had come over Tremble's face. "Look," she said. "One of those paddle wheel excursion boats is about to leave. Perhaps we should board it and go for a nice cruise. There's sure to be a good bar in there."

"It sounds wonderful," said Ennui. He pulled up his slacks and rubbed a cuff link. He felt like a new man in his old clothes. Ennui bought two tickets and gave one to Tremble.

"Go ahead and get on," said Tremble. "Get me a drink. I'll meet you in a second. I need to adjust my makeup."

"Okay," said Ennui. He walked up the gangway and disappeared inside the boat. A few minutes later he came out and saw that the gangway had been pulled up. He held two martinis.

"Good-bye," Tremble said, waving furiously. "I'm sorry to have to do this to you, Ennui, but I'm going away. I'm going home."

"I do believe you are sending me down the river," said Ennui. "That's rude."

Tremble was about to turn away, satisfied, but she suddenly remembered what she was going to ask Ennui before he went into the ape cage. The boat was pulling away.

"Ennui!" she yelled out. "Where did you get that money to pay the ape?"

"The lawyer forgot his briefcase in the swamp exhibit," said Ennui. "It was stuffed with cash, of course. I counted up to a million before I got bored. I was planning to surprise you with it, but it seems rather late now."

"Drat!" said Tremble. She crossed her arms and pouted. Ennui was growing smaller in the distance.

The calliope played and the paddle wheel slapped the water. The pouting, pigtailed figure of Tremble shrank and disappeared. Ennui looked down at the two martinis. Although he was sad to see Tremble abandon him like this, at least things had turned for the better. He was rich again, and he had his clothing back. And, he had not one, but two martinis in hand.

An old saying came into his head. "A martini in hand is worth two in the bush," he thought. "But what are two martinis in hand worth? Four in the bush?"

Perhaps it was time for Ennui to leave that sad old city of tumble-down shacks and termite-eaten mansions. He went out to the bow and let the breeze pass through his hair. He gazed at the huge oil refineries and rotting plantation houses sinking into the mud.

He mused further, "Four martinis are entirely too many to have hiding in a bush. They are bound to get warm before one could drink them all. Unless friends were around, of course. But then again, most people are just so stupid and bothersome..."

Deep beneath him, on the muddy bottom of the great river, catfish and eels swam in silence as the boat lurched overhead. They slid around sunken boats, cast-off furniture, and empty bottles. They lived among the human detritus that was blindly tossed into the river and washed out into the Gulf.

To Laura,
Miller,
and Henry

Tremble + Ennui
can be purchased through
bookstores in the U.S.